WESTERN WP PROMISES

Finding a Family

JUDY CHRISTENBERRY

H HARLEQUIN® WESTERN PROMISES

Recycling programs
for this product may
not exist in your area.

ISBN-13: 978-0-373-00373-0

Finding a Family

Printed in U.S.A.

www.Harlequin.com

Romance readers were sad to note the passing of **Judy Christenberry** in November 2013. Her writing career began with Harlequin Regency, and her varied and expansive talents eventually led her to write for several other lines, including Harlequin American Romance. Judy had a myriad of fans and extreme respect for her readers, working tirelessly to give them the type of story they loved, imbued with her signature warmth and humor. She will be dearly missed.

To my daughter, Christina, for her support, assistance and ideas. Without her, this book would never have been written.

Chapter 1

"Hank? You mooning over some girl?" Larry had to repeat his query before his boss realized that he'd asked him a question.

"What did you say, Larry?"

"I asked if you're mooning over some female? You're sure not paying attention to the cows today." Larry expected a funny answer. He and the boss bantered back and forth all the time.

Instead, he got a serious answer accompanied by concern on Hank's face. "I'm worrying about Dad."

"What's wrong with the old boss? Is he

sick?" Larry crossed his arms over his chest and frowned.

Hank Brownlee shrugged his shoulders. Life had changed since his mother had died last year. "I—I think he's depressed."

"Well, hell, Hank, his wife died. Of course he's sad."

"But that was over a year ago. I'm sad, too, when I think about Mom, but it's time to move on." Only his father hadn't. The older Brownlee had turned the ranch over to Hank and didn't seem to care what Hank did with the spread. He never asked about anything. He just sat and stared out the window. He wouldn't even eat if Hank didn't come in at night and cook.

"You'd better do something or he'll die, too."

Hank gave his friend a disgusted look. "I know that, Larry. But what? That's the problem. I've tried to spark his interest in anything but he just sits there. He won't budge."

"I think he needs a woman," Larry said with firmness.

Hank almost slugged his lifetime friend. "You're crazy. Dad's not interested in another woman."

"He might be if there was one around. Too

bad he doesn't live in a city. I heard there are lots of widow ladies out there looking for nice, mature gents to hook up with. He'd probably have a sweetie in no time. One already trained to cook and clean 'cause she's had a husband before."

With a sigh, Hank nodded. "I wouldn't mind having one of those around, too." When he saw Larry's face, he knew he'd misunderstood. "Wait a minute! I'm not looking for a wife. But I wouldn't mind someone else taking over the kitchen."

"Hey, you can kill two birds with one stone. Hire a nice widow to interest your dad *and* she could take care of the kitchen, and even the cleaning, too."

Hank gnawed on his bottom lip, looking at the suggestion from every angle. What could go wrong? Even if the woman irritated his dad, at least she might get a reaction out of him. That would be better than nothing. And he'd get some better meals.

"You know, Larry, I think you've got the right idea. I think I need to go widow-shopping!"

That evening, after a lackluster meal and the cleanup, which was worse than usual because he'd burned the meat loaf, Hank told his father good-night. He watched as his father shuffled down the hall to the master bedroom.

Hank had had several second thoughts about his decision, but his father's behavior tonight had strengthened his resolve to go through with his plan. There was no time to waste. He got out some paper and a pen and sat down at the kitchen table. What should he put in the ad?

By midnight, after much erasing, he'd come up with a simple advertisement.

Friendly widow needed to handle a male household. Cooking and cleaning required. Private bedroom and Sundays off. Send qualifications and photo to Brownlee Ranch, P.O. Box 512, Ashland, Colorado 80546.

He reread it several times. He'd get Larry to read it tomorrow. But he wouldn't mention his plan to Dad. He knew his father would condemn the idea, but Hank had to do something. He refused to lose his father, too.

Several weeks later he opened the day's mail with a sigh. Not much anticipation. None of the women who had contacted him thus far had seemed right. Most of them were too painted-up, the kind who would expect to be able to go to town two or three times a week. The closest town, Ashland, was twenty-five miles away. And it wasn't even a city.

Several of them didn't look as if they'd ever lifted so much as a finger for anyone, let alone run a household. Hank needed help; he sure didn't want someone else to take care of in addition to his dad.

He checked the postmark on the one letter he'd gotten today. Denver. Another city lady looking for a free ride he presumed.

When he ripped the envelope open, a picture fell out. He picked it up. Three people were in the picture, a lady around fifty, a beautiful young woman in her twenties and a toddler.

He liked the looks of the woman. Maggie. Nice name. Good, down-to-earth name. He scanned the letter. It was well-written and brief, and told him she enjoyed cooking and cleaning. She was perfect! Almost too good to be true. Hank decided to hire her. And as a bonus, he'd even allow the woman to let her daughter and grandson visit her at the ranch. Why not? Hank could afford to be generous, particularly if having the older woman around sparked his father's interest. Yep, this widow-woman would be just what his dad needed. Yeah, she would be perfect.

And her timing couldn't be better. Hank had promised a friend that he'd help with a round-up. The round-up would take Hank away from the ranch for a couple of days. Fearing to leave his dad alone, Hank had been afraid he'd have to renege on his promise. But now he'd have someone here to take care of his dad while he was away.

He quickly wrote out a letter of acceptance. His spirits were soaring. His dad was going to be taken care of and maybe even spark back to life. And hiring the widow would get Hank out of the kitchen. Hank had to admit he was a lousy cook. In fact, he'd been losing weight ever since his mom had died. And his dad was as frail as could be.

Hank didn't tell his father until the night before his departure. As the older man slowly rose and headed down the hallway, he stopped him. "Dad, I have a surprise for you."

"Don't want any surprises," he muttered, still moving.

"I've hired someone to cook and clean. She should arrive tomorrow, but I won't be here to show her around. I have to go to Ron Harper's place. Five of his guys are sick with the flu and I told him I'd pitch in." His father just snorted derisively as he continued down the hall.

"Dad, I hope you'll let this nice lady take care of you. Dad—I'll be back in a week."

Later, Hank gave more specific instructions to Larry, who was remaining on the ranch. "I left her first week's pay in an envelope for her." He handed Larry a white envelope. "Give it to her at the end of the week."

"What's her name?"

"Maggie. Good name, solid."

"Yeah. What did your dad say?"

"Nothing. He didn't seem to care. I hope I'm doing the right thing."

Larry leaned over and slapped him on the shoulder. "I'm sure you are. When is she coming?"

"Tomorrow, but I'll be up and out of here before she arrives. I left a note for her. Keep an eye on Dad for me."

"Will do."

Maggie Woodward pulled up in front of a nice ranch house with an old-fashioned broad porch. Tim could play out there no matter what the weather. She turned her car motor off and looked at the little boy still sleeping in the backseat.

She breathed a sigh of relief. She'd taken this job for Timmy's sake. She wanted him to have a country childhood like she had had.

Maggie had missed ranch life, but she'd gladly become a city girl when her husband took a job in Denver. She'd stayed home with Timmy, but after Derek's death, she'd gotten a secretarial job in Denver to support herself and her son and moved in with her aunt.

As she gazed around at her surroundings, Maggie wondered if her new employer would allow her to invite Kate to visit. She missed the older woman already and Timmy had cried this morning when they'd told Kate goodbye. So had Maggie.

With a sigh, she opened the car door and got out to take her son inside. It was late July, the hottest time in Colorado. She slid his little body toward her. He was sturdily built.

"Mommy?" the little boy muttered as he turned towards her body.

"It's all right, sweetie. Finish your nap." She climbed the steps to the back door, hoping no one would mind that she entered the house that way.

She heard something behind her and turned to see a young man hurrying out of the barn in her direction. She stood there in the afternoon sun, watching his approach.

"Howdy, ma'am. Are you Maggie?"

She smiled in relief. "Yes, I am, Mr. Brownlee."

"No ma'am. I'm not the owner. He's not here. He asked me to make you feel at… home. Who's he?" Larry asked, gesturing to the bundle of little boy in her arms.

"He's my son. May I take him in where it's cool? He's getting a little heavy."

"I'll take him." She shook her head so he stepped around her and held open the back door. "Did you mention to Hank that you'd be bringing him?"

She came to an abrupt halt in the kitchen and turned around. "Yes, I told him. Is there a problem?"

"I guess not," Larry muttered. "Uh, your bedroom is through here." He led her to the room behind the kitchen. After looking at the room, he said, "I guess Hank didn't have time to fix it up much," he muttered.

"That's all right," Maggie told him. The

welcome hadn't quite been what she was hoping for, but she could handle it.

Larry pulled down the grimy coverlet and discovered there were no sheets on the mattress.

"Can you find a sheet or quilt I can lay Timmy on?" Maggie quietly asked.

"Uh, yeah, sure." Larry had no idea where those things were. He found Mr. Brownlee sitting in his usual place in the living room. "Sir, where are the sheets?"

At first there was no change of expression. It was as if Carl Brownlee hadn't heard him. Then he frowned. "In the hall closet."

Larry hurried there and found a folded sheet. He grabbed it and headed for the back bedroom.

Carl actually came out of the living room. "You don't need to stay with me, Larry."

Larry turned around and backed toward the bedroom. "No, sir. This is for the housekeeper." Then he ducked into the room and laid the folded sheet on the bed.

Maggie, whose arms were aching with the weight of her son, breathed a sign of relief. "Thank you. If you'll just unfold it a little."

Larry did so and she laid her son down and gently covered him with part of the sheet.

"Who's that?"

She whirled around to see a frail old man leaning against the door frame. "That's my son, Timmy. I'll try to keep him out of your way."

"I like kids."

Maggie smiled, unaware of the effect of that smile. "I'm so glad to hear that."

Carl nodded slowly.

"Want me to help you carry your stuff in?" Larry offered.

"That would be nice if you have the time, but I can manage if you have work to do."

"Nothing that can't keep."

"I'll watch the child," Carl said, his gaze never leaving the little boy.

After she and Larry reached her car, she asked, "Is he okay?"

"I think Hank told you in his letter. His dad's been sad—I mean, depressed, since his wife died."

"When did she die?"

"A year ago last May."

"And part of my job is to take care of him?"

"Hank thought—I mean, he's not much of a cook. And he thought you could make Carl feel better."

Maggie flashed that beautiful smile again. "I understand, and I'll do my best."

By the time Larry left the house, after a well-cooked supper in a kitchen that already looked better, he was sure Hank had done the right thing. He didn't know why Hank had changed his mind about hiring a widow for his father, but the woman was a beauty and kind, too. And boy, could she cook.

She'd asked Carl what he liked to eat. His response had been his usual response, namely "nothing." But Maggie had told him what Timmy liked. The little boy asked for cookies, cake, hamburgers, all the things children like. To Larry's surprise, Carl had agreed with him.

Things were going well.

The bed in the room behind the kitchen was a single with an old mattress. Though Maggie longed for her queen-size bed in Kate's house, the smaller bed suited Timmy just fine. He'd fallen asleep soon after she'd put him down.

She returned to the kitchen to find Carl still sitting at the table.

"I'm sorry we didn't have any dessert tonight, Carl. You need fattening up, you know.

Would you like a cup of decaffeinated coffee while I make a chocolate cake for tomorrow?"

That seemed to be a strange idea to him, but he finally nodded.

She fixed two cups of coffee. Then, having checked the cabinets' contents, she pulled out what she needed. "You've got a lot of good equipment here. It's going to make my life easier."

She thought he wasn't going to answer, but he finally said, "My wife was a good cook."

"I bet she was. Tell me about her." She didn't rush him. Going about the business of making a cake, she waited for him to answer.

Finally, he began talking, slowly as if his voice was rusty. But his voice increased in volume and speed as if she'd started an avalanche. She listened, occasionally asking a question or making a comment. By the time the cake was baked and iced, he'd fallen silent at last. She looked up to find tears sliding down his cheeks.

She took out two saucers and cut two pieces of cake, a large one for him and a smaller one for her. She handed a plate to Carl. "We need to test the cake to see if it's good enough for Timmy."

He slowly picked up a fork and took a bite of the cake.

Maggie watched him closely. She hadn't had time to read the note the man's son had left her. She hoped she hadn't done anything wrong.

After he'd eaten several bites of cake, she said, "At first, it's hard to talk about someone who's gone. My husband died two years ago, just before Timmy turned two. But I found it got easier the more I talked about him."

"Yeah," Carl said, not looking up.

"I hope you'll tell me about some of the meals your wife cooked. I could try to make them again, though I'm probably not as good a cook as she was."

"The cake is good."

"I'm glad. I was so pleased to see the big back porch when we got here. I think Timmy will like playing back there, and I'll be able to keep an eye on him as I do my chores."

"I might—I might sit in the rocker sometimes, to keep him company."

"Oh, that would be wonderful! Timmy hasn't been around men much. It will be good for him to have a friend."

After she finished her cake, she began cleaning up the dirty dishes calmly and efficiently, keeping an eye on Carl without him realizing it. "What do you like for breakfast, Carl? Bacon and eggs?"

"Eggs and sausage," he said, as if he ate it every morning.

"Okay. At six-thirty?"

"That's when Hank will want it. I—I don't get up that early."

"Neither does Timmy. How about we eat around eight, until Hank gets home."

"Yeah, that'd be good. I really like this cake."

"Do you want another piece?"

"I'd better not. I'll have more tomorrow."

"Sure."

Carl shakily got to his feet.

Maggie stepped around the table and slid her arm under his. "Will you show me where your room is?"

They walked down the long hallway. Carl pointed out a room. "That's Hank's old room. It's still decorated for a little boy. I bet Timmy would like it." He pushed open the door.

Maggie knew Timmy would love it. But she didn't want him that far away from her. "It's very nice."

Carl gave her an unsure look. "This is my room and that's Hank's now," he said, pointing to the door opposite his. He pushed open the door to his room and Maggie saw she had a lot more work to do.

"This is a nice room. I'll get it cleaned up tomorrow."

Carl hesitated before he said, "That would be nice. I—I get tired."

"Because you haven't been eating properly, but we'll get you stronger."

Carl turned and put both his hands on her cheeks. "Maggie, I think you may be an angel."

"No, Carl," she said firmly. "I'm a friend. There's nothing angelic about me."

"Well, I'm glad you came."

"Me, too. Good night now." She slipped out of the room and down the hallway to her new bedroom.

Hank was dirty and exhausted. He'd worked from dawn to dusk and stayed up half the night guarding the herd. He wanted a hot shower and his bed, in that order. He'd worry about food in the morning.

He'd have to worry about his dad in the morning, too. He hoped the new housekeeper had arrived and was taking care of everything. Maybe his dad was already keeping her company. He snorted in derision. Sure, life was that easy.

He pulled in the driveway and was soon parked by the barn. He'd asked Larry to stay close until he got back, in case he'd hired an ax-murderer.

"Larry?" he called. His friend stepped out and greeted him.

"Welcome home, boss. Glad to see you."

"Thanks. Did she come?"

"Oh, yeah. And she's terrific. Best food I've had since—well, since your mom died."

Hank frowned. "And Dad? How's he dealing with her?"

"Like Mary's little lamb. He and Timmy just follow her everywhere."

"What? He's moving around? And who's Timmy?"

Larry took a step back. "Uh, she said you knew."

Hank knew it was all too good to be true. Harshly, he demanded, "Who's Timmy?"

"Maggie's little boy. I think he's three, almost four. Your dad plays with him."

"No!" Hank roared and turned on his heel, immediately striding toward his life-long home.

Larry was frozen for several seconds. Then he hurried after his friend.

Carl Brownlee was sitting in the rocking chair on the back porch. A little boy, Hank assumed the one in the picture, was standing at his father's knee, showing him a small car.

Carl looked up and smiled at Hank. That act alone almost knocked him off his feet. He couldn't remember the last time he saw his father smile.

"Dad?"

"Welcome home, son. Have you met Timmy?"

The little boy drew closer to Carl before he shyly said, "Hi."

"Hello," Hank said, frowning. Then he looked at his father again. "Where is she?"

"You mean Maggie? I believe she's putting in a load of laundry." Carl put his arm around Timmy. "She's a terrific housekeeper. And, man, can she cook!"

Hank felt as though his father had betrayed him. He'd been pleading with his father to eat, to talk, to smile. Now, a woman he hadn't hired—an imposter—had come and his father had gleefully done all three for her.

He ripped open the back door and entered the house. Larry waited on the porch with the elder Brownlee and the little boy.

In the laundry room, he discovered the young woman in the photograph. "I didn't hire you!" he exclaimed.

She straightened, her figure trim in snug-fitting jeans and a T-shirt. "I beg your pardon?"

"I didn't hire you. I hired Maggie!"

"Are you Hank?" she asked calmly.

"Yes! And you're not Maggie!"

"Yes, I am."

"No, you're not! Maggie was the older lady."

"That's my aunt Kate. The one in the picture with us?"

"I had no intention of hiring someone with a child. I won't have it. You have to leave!"

Maggie continued to load the dryer. She closed the lid and cleaned out the lint trap before starting the machine. Then she turned and walked past him without saying a word.

Chapter 2

Hank spun around and followed her to the small bedroom he'd planned for the house-keeper. He noted at once that it was spotless. He certainly hadn't left it that way. But that didn't matter.

"Did you hear me?"

She didn't answer, but she took a suitcase out of the closet and began packing. She looked over the lid at him. "It will take about an hour to get my things packed. Then we'll leave. I assume you will explain my leaving to your father?"

"Sure! I'll—I'll tell him you didn't like it

here." He was quite surprised by her compliance.

"But that would be a lie. Never mind. I'll explain everything to him when I say goodbye."

"What will you tell him?"

"The truth. That you fired me."

"You can't tell him that!"

She straightened and stared at him. "Why not?"

"It might upset him."

"Mr. Brownlee, whatever you tell your father, he'll be upset. For the first time in a year, he's eating good meals and gaining weight. He's sitting outside and enjoying the warm weather. He's taking an interest in the people around him. And he's very kind to Timmy. Sometimes he forgets and even calls Timmy Hank, but Timmy doesn't mind.

"If you want to fire me, that's your right. But I won't let that sweet man think I'm leaving on my own accord."

Hank glared at her. "Damn you!" he muttered and turned and left the room.

He stormed out onto the porch where three pairs of male eyes stared at him.

"What's wrong, son?" Carl asked.

"What's wrong? What's wrong? I didn't

hire a twenty-something with a child to be the housekeeper. I hired a nice fifty-year-old to cook and clean for us."

His father looked at him calmly and asked, "What difference does it make? Maggie is terrific at both and Timmy is keeping me company, aren't you, Timmy boy?"

Hank had no answer. When he'd left home a week ago, his father had been acting like a zombie. He was still too thin, but he was talking with the people around him. Carl was really interacting with the little boy, Larry, and obviously, Maggie.

Now what could he do?

He heard footsteps on the porch behind him. In a cool voice Maggie said quietly, "Timmy, I need you to come in, sweetie."

Timmy whispered to Carl, "I have to go."

He edged his way around Hank, as if he thought Hank was dangerous, and walked quickly to the back door. Then the little boy disappeared into the house.

"You scared the boy," Carl said in a chiding voice.

"I didn't mean to. But, Dad, they're going to have to go."

"Why?"

Hank couldn't come up with an answer.

"She cooks like an angel, she cleans like an army of people, and she's easy on the eyes, too. What's wrong with that?"

"She's too young for you, Dad!" Hank replied, anger in his voice.

"Mercy, boy, I'm not looking for a woman, but having a good-looking one around isn't a bad thing."

"Dad, you don't understand."

"Explain it to me then," the older man said. He sounded so reasonable, so much like the father Hank remembered…and had thought never to see or hear again.

"I want her to stay, son," Carl said softly.

Hank dropped his head. "Okay, Dad," Hank muttered. "You win."

He turned around and went into the house. He could hear activity in the spare bedroom. He stepped to the door.

Timmy was the first to see him. The little boy gasped as though he'd seen the devil himself. That got his mother's attention at once.

"Timmy?"

"It's him, Mommy!" The little boy grabbed her leg and hid behind her.

She straightened and confronted Hank, stare-for-stare. "Is there something else, Mr.

Brownlee? Do you want to search our luggage to be sure we're not stealing something from our luxury accommodations?"

Hank hated to be put in the wrong. Her sarcasm struck home. He hadn't even cleaned the room for her arrival. After all, she was the cleaning expert. But he knew he'd been a slacker there. "I apologize for not cleaning the room. I've been pretty busy with my dad."

"And you're here now because…"

She waited for him to fill in the blank.

With his cheeks red, Hank struggled to get the words out. "It's—it's not necessary for you to leave."

"Yes, I'm afraid it is." She returned to her packing, as if he were no longer there.

Hank drew a deep breath. "What I'm trying to say is I'm not firing you."

She ignored him.

"Damn it! My dad wants you to stay."

"We can't."

"Why not?"

"Because you've scared Tim."

Since she continued to pack, Hank realized he'd have to rectify his wrongs. He knelt down on one knee. "I didn't mean to scare you," Hank said, trying to soften the gruff

note in his voice. His attempt to hide his ir-
ritation failed miserably.

Suddenly the little boy was crying, and
his mother stopped packing to console him.

"What's wrong? What did I say wrong?"

Hank wanted to withdraw, to let them leave,
but his father had asked that they stay. What
could he do? "Look, can you at least stay another week, see if we can all get along? Dad
needs what you've been giving him. He needs
Timmy. I think Timmy is helping Dad get
well."

The little boy raised his head from his
mother's shoulder and sniffed. "He has lots
of boo-boos."

"Yes, he does. But he'll get better with your
help, Timmy. Will you and your Mommy stay
a little while?"

"I like it here…but you scare me."

Hank ground his teeth. "I promise I won't
scare you anymore." He felt he'd reached his
limit with the four-year-old. His gaze met
Maggie's, then looked away from the disap-
proval he saw in her blue eyes.

"What?" he asked, not specifying his question.

"We'll try it for a week. But you're on probation. I will not let my son live in constant terror!"

"I won't be around that much. This is a working ranch."

"I've only met Larry. You manage a ranch with one employee?"

"No, there are more hands, but right now my men are working on a neighbor's round-up. They'll be home tonight or tomorrow."

"Oh, I see. Do I cook for them, too?"

"No, they already have a cook."

"Uh, I think something is burning in here?" Larry called out.

Without a word, Maggie scooped up Tim and hurried to the kitchen, leaving Hank standing in her bedroom.

He followed her into the kitchen.

"It's all right, Carl," she said to his father. "It's just the marshmallow topping. I can redo it and have the sweet potatoes ready in no time."

"You actually made sweet potatoes with marshmallow topping?" Hank asked.

"Yes," she said without looking up. "Your father requested it."

"No wonder he doesn't want you to go."

"And what does that mean?"

"If you cater to his every whim, there's no telling what he'll ask for next."

She glared at him. "Why don't you join your father on the porch. I don't appreciate someone watching over my shoulder when I'm trying to prepare a meal."

"So you're throwing me out of my own kitchen?"

"Silly me. I thought it was your father's kitchen." She challenged him to say she was wrong.

With a scowl, he went out on the porch. He hadn't even realized Tim had already come out and was standing beside his father.

"What's Tim doing out here?"

The little boy tried to back away toward the kitchen door, but Carl had an arm around him. "He keeps me company. Sometimes we read books or play with a couple of Timmy's little cars. Other times, I tell him about you as a boy."

"Me?"

"You remember that time you got stuck in the hay barn?" Carl asked, a grin on his face.

"And a snake almost bit you!" Tim added, obviously too excited by the story to remember his fear of Hank.

"That's why Tim, here, shouldn't go climb the hay in the barn," Carl said. "Right, Timmy?"

"Right." The boy nodded his head several times.

"I see." When he'd left his dad last week, he would've sworn that his father couldn't have remembered his name, much less anecdotes about his son's childhood. Having the woman and the boy around had worked wonders for his father. "I'm glad you're feeling so much better, Dad," he said with a gusty sigh.

Carl narrowed his eyes. "You wonderin' why I didn't respond to all your attempts to make me change my ways?"

"I'm not the cook or housekeeper Maggie is, though I tried."

"It's not your fault son," the older man said. "You were out working all day. You needed your meals prepared for you, not having to prepare them yourself. I didn't blame you. Well, maybe occasionally when you burned everything to a crisp." He smiled.

Hank stared at his father. He was actually smiling. "I didn't mean to."

"I know that. No one would want that awful mess to eat."

Larry decided to pitch in. "Remember when he tried to make a cake, only he didn't follow the instructions? It was half-cooked and runny in the middle?"

Both Carl and Larry laughed at that story.

Tim tugged on Carl's sleeve. "What's runny?"

"Well, it means it wasn't cooked." When the little boy just stared at him, Carl tried again. "It was like water instead of cake."

Maggie opened the door and Tim ran to her. "Mommy, Hank made a water cake. It ran away!"

"I see…. Well, dinner is ready, if anyone's hungry."

All three men stood. Hank said, "I have to go clean up first."

"Don't be slow, boy, or I'll eat your share."

"There's plenty of food, Mr. Brownlee. Your father was just teasing." She moved back into the kitchen as they all followed her in.

"Do you call my father Mr. Brownlee?"

"No. He's asked me to call him Carl."

"Then you'd better call me Hank." He didn't wait for an answer. He went quickly to wash his hands so that he wouldn't miss the meal.

When Hank returned to the table, he was determined, despite the aroma he could smell all the way down the hall, to find fault with Maggie and her cooking.

Impossible.

He blamed that impossibility on the fact that he'd been eating round-up grub for too long. He'd been starving when he'd arrived home and been confronted with the widow mix-up, meaning Maggie. To make up for all the trouble she'd put him through he had helped himself to a double helping of the mashed potatoes with cream gravy on top, the sweet potatoes with marshmallows, the green beans and the T-bone steaks grilled to perfection. Not to mention the hot rolls.

Of course, that was the reason.

Then she brought out dessert.

Carl nodded in approval. "It looks just like Linda's carrot cake, Maggie. It's perfect."

Maggie smiled at such lavish praise. "Shouldn't you wait until you taste it, Carl?"

Hank wanted to refuse the cake. He didn't want to know that this woman could bake as well as his mother had. Somehow praising Maggie's prowess in the kitchen felt like a betrayal of his mother's memory.

"Your cake couldn't possibly be the same as the ones my mother used to bake. How would you—I mean, there are different reci-pes," Hank finally managed to get out.

"Yes, of course there are. But we found your mother's recipe book. It's wonderful, just full of great recipes she'd collected over the years. Your father has let me use it to make his favorite dishes, just like she did."

Looking around the table at the pleased expressions on his father, Larry and the little boy's faces, Hank decided to bide his time. He could air his differences with her later. For now Hank simply accepted a piece of cake and picked up his fork. The first bite stopped him in his tracks. It was the same cake his mother had always made. He couldn't deny it.

"This is wonderful, Maggie. I didn't think I'd ever taste a carrot cake as good as Lin-da's," Carl said.

"You still haven't, Carl," Maggie said with a smile. "This is Linda's cake. I made it, but it's her recipe."

"That's true. Thank you, Maggie."

Hank ground his teeth. He almost put down his fork. Almost.

"It sure is good," Larry added, smiling at Maggie.

Hank practically growled out loud. Was Larry flirting with his housekeeper?

"Yeah, Mommy, it's good."

Okay, he didn't mind if Timmy praised his mom. That was to be expected, but Hank did mind that Carl and Larry seemed to be complimenting Maggie to the heavens.

Looking up, he discovered everyone but Maggie was staring at him. "What?" he asked, frowning.

"Don't you like Mommy's cake?" Timmy asked, sounding as timid as before.

"Uh, yeah, it's good." He even smiled at the little boy, remembering Maggie's warning.

"I think you should take his cake away from him," Carl said to Maggie.

Astounded by his father's betrayal, Hank grabbed hold of his plate and glared at Carl. "Why would she do that?"

"Because that milk-toast compliment doesn't even begin to do this cake justice and you know it," Carl told him.

Hank knew his father was asking for a more…more high-falutin' compliment, but he was clean out of big words. "I like it, okay? You're right. It reminds me of Mom's cake."

To his surprise, it was Maggie who rescued him. "I'm more than happy with his praise,

Carl. I couldn't ask for more." She smiled at his dad…but not at him.

"I'm really tired, Dad. If you don't mind, I'll turn in early," Hank said, rising to his feet.

His father, instead of responding, spoke to Maggie. "I raised him better, Maggie, I promise."

"What did I do wrong?" Hank demanded.

"You excuse yourself to the lady of the house, son. Especially when she's just served you the best meal you've had in over a year."

"You mean the best meal I've had since Mom died, don't you, Dad?" Hank gulped down the lump he felt growing in his throat.

Grief over the loss of his mother took him by surprise. He knew his father was having difficulty with his mother's death, but he'd been fine. He'd kept busy. It was Dad who— he backed from the room, not even able to face his own thoughts, much less the consternation on the faces of the other people in the room.

No one spoke for several minutes. Then Larry said, "He's really tired. Didn't get much sleep, you know."

"Of course," Maggie said.

"I'd better go talk to him," Carl said, looking older almost within seconds.

Maggie reached out a hand to catch his. "No, Carl, I think it will be better to talk to him about it tomorrow morning. We have to respect Hank's grief." Carl nodded in agreement and returned to the table and sat down.

"Do you remember that first night, when you talked about Linda? The words tumbled out of you as if they'd been blocked inside you for months. Has Hank ever talked like that about his mom since she passed?"

Carl slowly shook his head, a frown on his face.

"I think the best thing you can do is give him some space… And besides, just because you're happy with me doesn't mean Hank is. Perhaps it will be best if Timmy and I leave."

"No, Maggie, I'll insist—"

"But that doesn't work, Carl. Didn't Hank insist that you stop mourning your wife and be happy?"

"Yeah, he did," Carl said slowly.

More softly, she asked, "Did it work?"

Carl stared at the floor. "You know it didn't."

Maggie patted Carl's shoulder. "It isn't your fault, Carl."

"I guess you're right," he conceded. "Which gets me to thinking. If you helped me to open up about my feelings maybe you could do the same for Hank."

The old man's expression brightened with the thought that he might just have hit upon a compelling reason to persuade Maggie to stay.

Chapter 3

It took effort for Hank to pry his eyes open the next morning. He'd barely undressed before he hit the bed and fell asleep last night. This morning, he noticed the clean sheets and the tidiness of his room.

Somehow, instead of feeling good about the changes, he felt violated. He felt as if *she* had invaded his space. He hadn't asked for anyone to take care of his room. He had hired her to cook and look after his dad, not to invade his privacy and to mess with his things.

He'd make sure that *she* knew her duties this morning. As soon as she got up he'd set things straight. She probably slept late every morning. He'd probably still have to fix his own breakfast.

He rolled out of bed and groped on the floor for the clothes he'd taken off the night before. Everything else was even dirtier because he hadn't had time to do laundry before he left. With his eyes only half open, he continued to feel around on the floor for his clothes.

They weren't there!

Okay, maybe his dad had come in and picked them up and put them on the only chair in his room. They weren't there, either.

He whirled around, scanning the room. Everything was neat and tidy, no dust on the chest of drawers, no dirty clothes piled in the corner. Crossing to the dresser, he pulled open a drawer. Stacks of clean underwear and T-shirts met his gaze.

He sheepishly took out a pair of briefs and a T-shirt. Then he opened another drawer and found a stack of clean jeans. In the closet he found numerous shirts hanging neatly in a row.

When he was dressed, he headed for the kitchen. He'd overslept this morning. It was already eight-thirty. He assumed that he would have the kitchen to himself, but he found his father, Timmy and Maggie sitting at the table.

As soon as Maggie saw him standing at the door, she jumped to her feet. "Good morning, Hank. Come have a seat."

Before he could move, she'd filled a mug of fragrant coffee and put it at his place. With a scowl he moved to his chair and pulled it out. He hadn't looked at his father.

Maggie didn't return to the table. Instead, she began cooking pancakes. Once she had the batter on the grill, she moved to the microwave oven and turned it on. In no time, he had a plateful of pancakes and bacon.

His father passed the butter and syrup. "Here you go, son. You haven't lived until you've tasted Maggie's pancakes."

Before Hank could taste the pancakes, which he was sure would be run-of-the-mill, he had to clear up last night's fracas.

"Dad, I'm sorry about last night, but—"

"Don't worry about it, son. You were over-tired from the round-up. Many a time your mother would say she didn't want to see me after a round-up until I'd showered and slept for a day or two."

Hank couldn't believe how casually his father had spoken of his mother. They'd avoided talking about her ever since she'd died. His father had turned into a zombie and he'd held back his own grief so as not to burden his father.

"Go ahead, boy, eat your pancakes before they get cold."

Hank gave his dad a nod, not sure he could speak without letting everyone know how upset he was. But even though it was painful to talk about his mother's death, it made him feel good to know his father hadn't forgotten his mother.

When he put the first bite of pancake in his mouth, he realized there was nothing run-of-the-mill about these pancakes. They tasted as good as a regular cake.

"Are you sure these aren't dessert?" he asked without thinking.

"Told you they were good," Carl said with great glee.

Hank continued to eat, refusing to look at Maggie or his father. When he'd gobbled down the stack of pancakes on his plate, Maggie calmly asked him, "Do you want some more?"

"No! I mean, no thank you."

"Are you sure? I have leftover batter that will just go to waste."

"Fine. I can eat some more if you have the batter," Hank agreed. He kept his head down until Tim slid out of his chair and patted Hank on the knee.

"Yes, Timmy? What is it?"

"Do you have a headache? That's what Mommy has when she won't talk."

Hank looked at Maggie before he answered the little boy. "Uh, yeah, maybe I do have a headache. Which, uh, reminds me. I couldn't find the clothes that I took off last night."

His father started to answer, but Maggie beat him to it. "Your father was concerned about you. When he checked on you, he picked up your dirty clothes and took them to the laundry room to save me a trip," she said and smiled.

"I don't need you to do my laundry or clean my room or…whatever else you do. I can take care of myself. I hired you to take care of my dad."

"But—" Maggie began.

"There's no need for discussion! I have to get to the barn and see about my men."

"Uh, boy, I gave them the day off," Carl said, knowing this would further upset his already agitated son.

Hank stared at his father. "You did what?

Damn it to hell! Dad, you turned the ranch over to me a year ago. I thought I was supposed to be in charge!"

"I was trying to help. They're all exhausted, just like you. I thought they deserved the day off."

Hank didn't speak. He got up and strode out of the kitchen as if he were being chased.

Maggie watched him go, grateful that he'd eaten a good breakfast. She'd noticed when he'd cataloged what she shouldn't do for him that he hadn't mentioned her cooking. She'd thought his dad had been a hard case! Carl was a walk in the park compared to Hank.

"Maggie, I hope Hank didn't offend you. I don't know what's got into that boy."

"I think he's working through his grief, Carl. He's glad that you've overcome yours, but he needs the chance to work through his feelings."

Carl frowned. "Do you think so? He sure gave me a funny look when I talked about Linda this morning."

"Yes, but I still think you should continue. He's buried his grief for too long. At least he didn't object to eating my cooking."

Carl laughed. "He'd have to be dead to refuse your cooking."

"Mommy, is Hank mad at me?" Timmy asked.

"No, sweetie. He's upset that his mother died, that's all. You know, we felt really sad when your dad died."

"Yeah," Timmy said slowly, his little face screwed up, as if he were thinking very hard. "I could give him one of my cars. That would make him happy."

Carl held his arms out to Timmy. "Come give me a hug, Timmy."

With a nod from his mother, Timmy did as Carl suggested. Afterwards, Carl said, "That's a real generous offer, giving Hank one of your cars, but adults are different. We will have to be really patient with him."

"Okay," Timmy said, but he didn't look particularly enlightened.

"It's all right, Timmy," Maggie said softly. "Why don't you take Carl outside while I clean the table."

After the duo had disappeared to the back porch, Maggie cleared the table and thought about Hank. Not that she was interested in him. No, she didn't intend to remarry. The pain was too great when the marriage ended, whatever the reason. She wasn't willing to risk that again.

But Hank, like his father, was suffering from burying pain deep inside him. She would've done the same when her husband died if she hadn't had Kate to prod her out of her depression, reminding her that Timmy needed her.

If she could do the same for Hank, it would be like passing on the serenity Kate had helped her find.

After she'd loaded the dishwasher, Maggie thought about what she could do. Almost as if she were guided by Linda's hand, she reached for the cookbook Carl had loaned her. Slowly turning the pages, she came upon a well-worn recipe. Somehow she just knew that it was the recipe for Hank's favorite cookies.

With a smile, she took down a mixing bowl. Soon she put a batch of cookies into the oven. Oatmeal raisin were Timmy's favorite, too.

Hank didn't come in for lunch. But he wanted to. It seemed he could smell the enticing aroma of Maggie's good cooking all the way in the barn. Larry didn't demonstrate any of his reluctance. He went in for lunch without a qualm.

Of course, Larry had also backed his dad's

decision to give the men a day off. Not that Hank thought the decision was wrong. It was just that he should've had the opportunity to…he was being foolish.

Hank ran his hand through his hair. Why was he acting this way? He'd hired Maggie to make things right in the house. Then he'd forbidden her to do his laundry or clean his room. Was he crazy?

Maybe so.

An hour or so later, Larry came back into the barn. "What are you doing, Hank?"

Hank sat down on a bale of hay, staring glumly into the distance. "Nothing."

"Why didn't you come in for lunch?"

"Because I couldn't face Dad or Maggie."

Larry looked alarmed. "Uh-oh, what did you do?"

"I acted like a fool. Dad was praising Maggie to the skies, like he'd completely forgotten Mom. Then he casually mentioned her in the next breath."

"Yeah, I've noticed him talking about Linda a lot nowadays. I think that's good for him." After pausing, Larry said slowly, "I've never heard you talk about your mom."

"Damn it! I don't spill my guts every other minute, Larry. I'm a man!"

Larry shrugged and walked away, muttering under his breath, "Just a thought."

Not one Hank wanted to consider. But, as if a dam had burst inside of him, images of his mother ran through his mind. When she'd decorated the house for Christmas, or made him a special snack when he'd come home from school. Or when she tended him when he had the measles, or had hurt himself playing football.

And then there were all the times she'd read him stories before he went to sleep each night when he was a little boy.

He loved his dad, and they'd spent many hours working together. But he and his mom had shared a special bond.

Tears filled his eyes, and he was glad Larry had gone off somewhere else. He hastily wiped the tears away. He missed his mom, his best friend.

He stood and paced the aisle in the barn. He had to get control of himself. He couldn't let anyone see him as weak as he felt right now.

When Hank came in for dinner, he avoided looking at Maggie. She didn't know if that was a good sign or a bad one. With Carl's help she'd worked extra hard to make Hank's favorite meal. Since he had missed lunch, Maggie figured Hank wouldn't refuse to eat dinner.

As she put the dishes on the table, she covertly studied Hank. He looked at each dish and then stared at his father. He said nothing. Carl asked him what he'd done all day.

"I worked," Hank said.

"Everything okay?" Carl asked.

"Fine!" Hank snapped.

"Carl, could you fill Timmy's plate for him?" Maggie hurriedly asked. If she didn't do something, Hank would leave the table without eating anything.

"Mrs. Washburn came over this afternoon," she added. "She had heard that you hired a housekeeper. She wanted to make sure I wouldn't be any competition for Carl's heart. You didn't tell me you had a secret admirer, Carl."

That should change the subject.

"Who? Me?" Carl roared. "Sue Washburn is interested in me? Not a chance. Her husband was the most miserable man I've ever met. We all figured when he died it was because he couldn't stand living with Sue any longer."

"Dad! You shouldn't say such things."

"Well, it's true. The woman can't even cook."

"She might learn for you, Carl," Maggie teased.

"Don't need her to. We've got you, Maggie. You're as good a cook as Linda." Carl didn't notice his son's frown, but Maggie did.

"You should meet my Aunt Kate. She's an even better cook than I am, and she's charming, too."

"I love Aunt Kate!" Timmy said with a chuckle. "She's fun."

"Yes, she is," Maggie said, hoping the men wouldn't notice her wistful expression.

"Well, why don't we invite her for a visit?" Carl asked.

"Let's wait until I get my new bed set up. I don't think Kate, Timmy and I could manage on the single bed I have now."

"I thought you said it was coming right away," Carl said.

"I thought it was. But they called and told me delivery had been delayed for a week."

Hank cleared his throat. "If I drove into town to pick it up, could it be ready for tomorrow?" he asked.

"I—I don't know. I didn't ask that question."

"Call them in the morning. If it can be picked up, I'll go after I get the men started on their jobs."

"That's very kind of you to offer, but it's not necessary."

"I feel guilty enough for not cleaning the room. Maybe this will make up for it."

"Thank you, Hank. That would be nice."

"That's thoughtful of you, son," Carl added.

"Let's not overdo it, Dad," Hank growled.

"Okay. What's for dessert, Maggie?"

Maggie wished she could hide the cookies, but she had nothing else to offer them for dessert. And Carl expected dessert. "Uh, I baked cookies today. Will that be okay?"

"Of course it will," Carl said with enthusiasm.

Hank stared at her. "What kind of cookies?" he asked.

"Um, well, I wanted a healthy treat for Timmy, and I found a recipe in your mother's cookbook that looked—"

That was as far as she got before Hank bolted out the back door.

"You made the oatmeal cookie recipe,

didn't you?" Carl asked. "I should've warned you."

"I was hoping it would bring back good memories for Hank," Maggie said softly. "I wasn't trying to hurt him."

"Can't be helped. Bring on the cookies, right, Timmy?"

"Right," Timmy agreed with a giggle.

Maggie was still up when she heard Hank come into the kitchen. It was just a little after ten. When she hurried to the kitchen in her robe, she found him with his hand in the cookie jar.

"I'll be glad to put on some coffee to go with those cookies," she offered softly.

"That's too much trouble just for me," he growled.

"I'd enjoy some coffee, too."

"Then why didn't you make some already?"

"Because making a pot of coffee just for me seemed…frivolous."

"Then by all means make a pot of coffee." He pulled out a chair and sat down at the table.

Maggie got a saucer from the cabinet for his cookies. She added a few more cookies to it and slid it in front of him. Then she started the coffee perking.

"Aren't you having any of these healthy cookies?" Hank asked.

"Absolutely," she said. Maggie retrieved a small plate from the cabinet, placed three cookies on it and set the plate on the table before her.

"Is that all you're eating?"

"I had a few after dinner. I can't afford to eat too much late at night. It puts on pounds, you know."

She felt his gaze as it went slowly from her toes to her head and shivered.

"I don't think you have to worry," he drawled, looking away.

"Thank you." The light on the coffeepot came on and she got up and poured two cups. Then she sat down at the table again.

They both ate in silence. Finally, Maggie said, "I love this recipe. I hadn't run across it before."

He raised one eyebrow and continued to eat.

"Well, I've certainly made oatmeal cookies with raisins, but I wouldn't have thought to add nuts and chocolate chips."

"My mother made them for more than twenty years."

"She must've been a terrific mother," Maggie said softly.

But she didn't fool Hank. He stood, politely thanked her for the late snack, and stalked down the hall to his bedroom.

Okay, so he wasn't as easy to help as his dad had been. She should've known better.

Maggie got up early enough the next morning to have breakfast ready for Hank before he went out to the barn.

When he arrived in the kitchen, she could read the shock in his face. "I didn't think you'd be up this early."

"I've been lazy the past week because there was no one up to eat this early in the morning. But this is my job, Hank, remember?" She poured him a hot cup of coffee and slid a plateful of scrambled eggs and bacon in front of him. Then she put a pan of homemade biscuits on the table.

Rather than sitting down with him, she worked at the sink, keeping her back to him. She didn't want him going out to work without a good breakfast in him. And she sensed that her presence at the table might annoy him. She realized that his presence in the kitchen had an unsettling effect on her as well.

She turned around when he cleared his throat. He was standing by the table.

"Thanks for the great breakfast, Maggie."

"You're welcome. Will you be able to drive into town today to pick up my bed?"

"Yeah. I'll come back in an hour."

"I don't think anyone will be at the store before nine."

"Okay, I'll be back at nine." Then he disappeared out the back door.

Maggie moved to the window to watch his long strides as he walked toward the barn. He was a strong man, which made helping him all the more difficult. Hank Brownlee was definitely a challenge, but Maggie loved a good challenge, especially such an attractive one.

She put in a load of laundry and mopped the kitchen floor. Then she made blueberry muffins for Timmy and Carl. Just as the muffins came out of the oven, her little boy came to the kitchen in his pajamas, rubbing his eyes.

"Timmy, I think you forgot to get dressed. I laid out your clothes for you."

"Hmmm..." Timmy mumbled. "I'm hungry."

"And you can eat as soon as you get dressed," she said firmly. "Run along and put on your clothes."

Carl came in as Timmy left. "Hey, Timmy boy, where you going?"

"I have to get dressed," Timmy said with a pout, but he continued on his way.

"He could eat in his pajamas, Maggie. I wouldn't mind," Carl assured her.

"I appreciate that, but it's better if he sticks to a routine."

"I suppose so. Linda always liked things that way. I remember one time when Hank rebelled. He went off without breakfast because she refused to feed him until he did as he ought. I don't know which one suffered the most. Linda worried about him all day.

"When he finally dragged in, he apologized at once. Which was a good thing 'cause Linda was gonna apologize to him!" Carl recalled with a laugh.

"I'm sure it was hard on her," Maggie agreed, but she was remembering how hard it had been this morning, making sure Hank ate his breakfast before he went out to work.

She put breakfast on the table. Then she stepped around the corner to their room.

"Timmy? I made blueberry muffins for breakfast. You'd better get to the table before they get cold."

Timmy was still in his pajamas in the middle of their small bed. "I don't want to get dressed."

Maggie came over and felt his cheeks. "Aren't you feeling well, Timmy?"

"I hurt, Mommy," he said, raising his head.

"Where do you hurt, Timmy?"

"My head hurts."

She already knew he was running a high fever, and the tears in his eyes convinced her. She piled up the pillows on the bed and laid him down upon them. Then she pulled the sheet and a light blanket up over him. "Let me feed Carl. Then I'll bring you some breakfast."

"In bed?" Timmy asked, disbelief in his voice.

"Yes, when you're sick, you get breakfast in bed," Maggie told him with a smile.

Back in the kitchen, she explained that Timmy wasn't feeling well.

"What do you think it is?" Carl asked.

"It's hard to know. He may be coming down with a summer cold," Maggie said.

"Well, you go ahead and take him some

breakfast. I have everything I need. Just tell him I want him to get well."

"I will, Carl. Thanks, and you just call if you need something." She fixed a plate for Timmy and carried it into her little boy. She settled down beside him and fed him his breakfast. He didn't finish it all, but he did a fair job. Then she tucked him in again and told him to rest.

He was asleep before Maggie left the room. Which worried her even more. Usually Timmy was filled with energy.

After cleaning up the kitchen, Maggie went in search of the elder Brownlee. She found Carl out on the back porch. She stepped outside to tell him Timmy was sleeping.

"Do you need to take him to the doctor? You could ride into town with Hank and get Timmy looked at."

"It depends on how he's feeling. If his fever rises in the next hour, I might. Do y'all have a doctor you go to?"

"Of course. I'll give him a call if you want me to."

"Thank you, Carl."

She hurriedly fixed a lunch that could be heated up if she wasn't back from town in time. Then she called about her bed. The store agreed she could pick it up this morning.

When she returned to her room and felt Timmy's cheeks, she was alarmed to realize how hot he felt.

She went out to the porch. "Carl? Could you call that doctor? Timmy's very hot."

Carl hurried in to the phone. In no time, he had an appointment for Timmy at eleven o'clock.

"Can we get there by then?"

"Sure, if Hank comes on time. It's only an hour and a half drive."

"You don't think he'll mind, do you?"

"Mommy?" Timmy's distressed call just barely reached Maggie's ear. She rushed into the bedroom.

Timmy was sitting up, holding his stomach. "I don't feel good, Mommy."

"Sweetie, are you going to throw up?"

The little boy nodded, a scared look on his face.

She scooped him up and took him to the bathroom, getting him there just in time. Timmy lost his breakfast in convincing fashion. She'd washed his face and carried him back to bed, just as they heard Hank come into the house.

"Maggie, is your bed ready to be picked up?" he called.

After putting Timmy back to bed, she went into the kitchen, followed by Carl. She only hoped Hank wouldn't object to their change in plans.

Chapter 4

"Timmy's sick?" Hank asked, concern in his voice.

"Yes. He—he just lost his breakfast, and he's running a high fever," Maggie explained. "Your father called a doctor in town who agreed to see him at eleven today. I was hoping you wouldn't mind taking us."

Hank watched her carefully. All he could see was worry about her son. It reminded him of his mother. "Uh, sure, that will be fine." He looked at his dad. "Did you call Doc Bragan?"

"Yep."

"Okay. I'll go clean out my truck a little.

Then we can go." After Maggie nodded her assent, Hank hurried to his truck. He seldom had a passenger and he'd gotten lazy about keeping it clean. When he'd thrown out the trash, he went back to the house. He called to Maggie, and she came out of her room with Timmy wrapped in a blanket, asleep in her arms.

"Here, let me take him. You're not big enough to carry him like that." He scooped the little boy up into his arms. "Why don't you get a pillow? You can make him more comfortable like that."

With a shaky smile, she hurried back into her room to get a pillow.

Hank noticed how hot Timmy was. "Did you give him some children's aspirin?"

"I was afraid to. We'll just wait and see what the doctor says. I'm going to wet down a cloth and keep it on his head. That will help," she assured him.

He thought she was trying to convince herself more than him. He simply nodded. His father came in as he reached the back door.

"How's the little guy?"

"He's hot, Dad. It's a good thing you called the doctor."

"Yeah, I thought it might be."

Maggie came to join them. She looked worried.

"He'll be fine, Maggie," Carl assured her, squeezing her shoulder.

"Of course he will," she agreed. "Your lunch is in the refrigerator. All you have to do is put it in the microwave for three minutes when you're ready to eat. There's enough for Larry, too, so you won't have to eat alone."

"Thanks, Maggie, but you shouldn't have worried about me," Carl protested.

Maggie just nodded, her gaze fixed on her son. "I think we'd better go," Maggie said.

"Right," Hank agreed and strode toward the door.

Maggie hurried forward to open it for him since his hands were full, holding her son. Carl followed behind to hold the door open for Maggie.

"Give me a call after you see the doctor," Carl ordered.

Maggie nodded. "I have my cell phone."

Once they were settled in the truck, there was nothing more for Maggie to do except watch her son. Her panic increased. This was the first time since her husband's death that Timmy had been sick and Maggie didn't want to face the possibility of losing her son.

"What's going on?"

The sudden question from Hank awakened Maggie from the downward spiral of dismal thoughts in which she'd been drowning. "What?" she asked, jerking her head up.

"I asked what's going on. You seemed to be unhappy. Are you worried about Timmy?"

"Of course I am. He's my only child."

"So, if you had six, it wouldn't bother you as much?"

She glared at him. "Of course it would!"

"He's going to be fine, Maggie."

"How do you know?" Her anger was mixed with eagerness to be reassured.

"I don't know for sure, but I remember my dad telling me how upset Mom would get when I was sick, but I always got well. I'm sure the same will be true for you and Timmy."

After a moment of silence, Maggie said, "Yes, all right, I'm overdoing the worrying, aren't I?"

"I think so. And if it would help, I'd join in," he assured her with a warm smile. "But it won't. So let's just wait until we see the doctor."

Maggie drew a deep breath and leaned

back against the car seat. "Okay. How much longer?"

"About half an hour. Why don't you take a little nap? You may be up late tonight."

Maggie nodded and let her eyes drift closed.

Hank kept his gaze on the road until several minutes had passed. Then he sneaked a look at Maggie and the little boy beside her. It was like looking into a mirror that reflected his life. Anytime he'd been sick, his mother had immediately been at his side. Nothing his father or Maggie could have done would have brought his mother back to him more than seeing Maggie hovering over her sick child.

He spent the rest of the drive in peace, listening to softly playing music on the radio, as his passengers slept.

When he reached the store where Maggie had ordered her bed, he put the truck in Park, but left the motor running. Working as quietly as he could and with help from one of the salesmen, he loaded the bed in the back of his pickup.

He slipped back into the cab of the truck and discovered Maggie was awake.

"Are you doing all right?"

"Yes, thank you."

"How's Timmy?"

Maggie leaned over and felt Timmy's forehead. "He's still hot, but maybe not quite so much."

"We'll be at the doctor's office in fifteen minutes," Hank told her.

When they reached the doctor's office, Hank gathered the small boy in his arms and carried him inside. The nurses greeted him with affection, looking curiously at the boy in his arms. The nurses then showed them into the doctor's office.

"Welcome, Hank. I didn't know you'd married, much less started a family. Let's have a look at your boy," Dr. Bragan said, standing to pull back the blanket.

"He's older than I expected. You been keeping secrets from me, Hank?"

Maggie stepped forward. "This isn't Hank's son. I'm the Brownlee's new housekeeper and Timmy is my son."

Hank was amazed at the disappointment he felt at having to disclaim Maggie and her child. He'd liked the momentary feel of being a father and a husband. And the thought of being Maggie's man gave him a funny feeling in his stomach.

"Well, welcome. I'm Dr. Bragan."

"Maggie Woodward, doctor. And this is my son, Timmy. I appreciate you seeing us on such short notice."

"Hank and Carl are my special patients. If you're from their ranch, you're welcome here. Now, let's have a look at Timmy. How old is he?"

"He just turned four. He woke up this morning not feeling well. He's been running a fever, and he threw up his breakfast."

"Edith, come in here," Dr. Bragan called.

Immediately, an older woman in starched white appeared at the door. "Yes, Doctor?"

"We need to make a file on Timmy here, Timmy Woodward. And take his temp."

"Yes, Doctor." She handed Maggie a clipboard and a pen. "Please fill out these forms while I take a look at Timmy."

Five minutes later, Maggie had filled out the forms and Edith had taken Timmy's temperature and done a quick examination.

Dr. Bragan, who had taken Hank into his office for a chat about Carl, Maggie suspected, came back into the room, Hank following him.

"Well, Edith, what do you think?"

Maggie held her breath as well as her child, waiting for Edith's pronouncement.

She'd made several mutters as she'd looked at Timmy.

"Chicken pox," Edith said succinctly.

Maggie gasped in surprise. The doctor looked first at Edith and then at Maggie. Finally, he turned to Timmy who was sitting on the examining table, his mother's arms around him.

"Mind if I have a look, young man?" the doctor asked Timmy, who, at his mother's whispered prompting, nodded.

After a couple of minutes, Dr. Bragan agreed with Edith's evaluation. "I'm afraid Edith is right," he said, looking at Maggie. "I assume you've had chicken pox?"

"Yes, I have. I don't know about Hank, though," Maggie said, shifting her gaze to Hank.

"Me? Oh, I had them," he assured her.

"I'm going to have Edith get you a pamphlet on caring for someone with chicken pox. Mostly you'll need oatmeal baths and calamine lotion and lots of patience. You can also use some children's aspirin for the fever."

"All right."

"Here's a prescription for the oatmeal baths. You can pick them up at the drugstore on your way out of town. You can get the calamine lotion there, too. And call us if there are any complications. Keep him in bed until his fever is completely gone. He'll want to get up long before that, but it's important for him to have complete bed rest."

"Yes, doctor," Maggie said, wondering how she would manage to keep her energetic child in bed when he began to feel a little better.

When they got to the drugstore, Hank offered to go in and pick up what they needed, but Maggie asked if he would mind staying in the truck with Timmy. In the store, she added several new coloring books, a new pack of crayons, a puzzle book and a new storybook to her purchases.

When she returned to the truck, afraid Hank would be impatient with her shopping, she found him calm.

"Need to go anywhere else before we head for home?"

"No, thank you. I'm sorry I took so long."

"No problem. Did you find some things to entertain the little guy?"

"Yes. I thought that would be a good idea since I can't sit beside him all day."

Hank remained silent for several minutes

and she wondered if she'd offended him. Then he said, "I think you should call your Aunt Kate and see if she can come help you out for a few days. We talked about her coming to visit once you got your bed."

"Yes, but… I wouldn't have time to visit with her while I'm doing my job and taking care of Timmy."

"I thought she'd help you with Timmy. And she can stay as long as you want. There wouldn't be any need for her to rush off. She doesn't hold down a job, does she?"

"No, she's a retired teacher."

"Then call and ask her. We can pay her for helping you out."

"No, that's not necessary," Maggie said, knowing what her aunt's reaction to such a suggestion would be. She dug in her purse beside the sleeping Timmy and pulled out her cell phone.

"Aunt Kate? It's me, Maggie. No, everything's fine. Well, sort of. Timmy's got the chicken pox. My boss doesn't mind if you come visit and…are you sure you don't mind? You can stay as long as you want so we'll have time to visit." After another pause, she said, "Thank you, Aunt Kate. I can't wait, either."

"She's coming?" Hank asked.

"Yes, in the morning. Thank you, Hank, for letting me call her."

"Don't put a halo on me. I like my creature comforts, just like any man."

Maggie frowned at him. "So it was all for you?"

"Yeah," Hank returned, staring straight ahead.

"I should've known," Maggie muttered and crossed her arms over her chest, staring out the window.

"Did you upset Maggie?" Carl asked his son as he stepped out onto the back porch.

"Yeah," Hank confessed.

"Why? She's got enough to worry about with Timmy being sick."

"Because, Dad, I didn't want her feeling beholden to me. That would just give her one more thing to worry about. Now, she doesn't feel she owes me anything."

"I'm not sure about your thinking, boy, but at least you had good intentions. That bed makes her room look pretty small, doesn't it?"

"Yeah, I noticed that. I was thinking maybe Timmy would like my old room. It's not too far away from his mom's and the kid is old enough to have his own room."

"That's a good idea. Have you suggested it to Maggie?"

"I don't dare. She's really overprotective when it comes to the boy." Hank wasn't sure why he was so worried about that. He just knew he didn't want Maggie feeling that way about him.

"Then I'll suggest it to her," Carl said and walked back into the house.

Hank didn't expect Maggie to accept the offer. The apron strings were firmly tied between her and her son. It worried Hank a little. Poor little guy wouldn't have much chance to grow up until those strings were cut. Maybe that was what Hank could do for him.

With that thought, he stepped off the porch and headed for the barn. An idea had popped into his head that needed checking out.

"Carl, that's a very generous offer, but I think I still need to be close to Timmy. We'll be just fine, in this room together."

"Whatever you say, Maggie, but if you change your mind, let me know. When is your aunt coming?"

"In the morning. I appreciate your letting her come. It will make such a difference for Timmy and me."

"Happy to do it. Is there something I can do for you now?"

Maggie looked over her shoulder to where Timmy was sleeping in their new bed. "No. I bought this today," she said, pulling out a monitoring device. "I can work in the kitchen, but with this I can hear Timmy the minute he wakes up." She put the batteries in both units. Hanging one on the bed, she led Carl out of her room to the kitchen. She set the other unit on the cabinet and turned up the volume. Timmy could be heard breathing.

"That's a wonderful idea, Maggie."

"Thank you. Now I can bake a cake for Aunt Kate...and dessert tonight," she added with a smile when she noted Carl's disappointment.

"Oh, good. I've kind of gotten used to having dessert."

"I'm glad you have. You've put on some weight since I got here and it looks good on you."

"I'm feeling a lot better, too. I'm going to have to go back to work, soon."

"Won't that upset Hank?" Maggie asked, frowning.

"Probably, but it won't be the first time I've upset him. He'll get over it. How old is your Aunt Kate?"

Surprised by the change of subject, Maggie said, "Aunt Kate? She's fifty-four. Why?"

"Just wondered. She looks kind of young in that picture of the three of you."

Maggie smiled. "She is young to have retired, but she had put in thirty years of teaching. With her husband's military pension and her teaching pension, she doesn't have to work any more. She thought about doing some traveling, but then she stayed home to help me and Timmy."

"She likes to travel?"

"Yes. She used to go on trips every summer." Maggie began organizing what she needed for the cake she was going to make, moving about the kitchen while she talked.

"I thought about traveling. But I thought I couldn't be replaced here on the ranch. Linda's death taught me a lot of things. One of them is that Hank is a pretty good manager. The other thing is that traveling or anything else is no fun alone."

"Kate has traveled alone occasionally, but

she usually finds a girlfriend who wants to travel, too."

"That's probably a good idea. Maybe I'll find a girlfriend, too," Carl said with a grin, and Maggie laughed at the suggestion. "I think I'll go out to the barn and see if I can help Hank for a while. Is dinner at the usual time?"

"Yes. If you're not back by then, I'll ring the bell," Maggie assured him.

Carl strolled out to the barn where he found his son cleaning out the stalls. "Need any help?"

Hank looked up in surprise. "Sure, if you feel like it."

Carl started to do the familiar work, a grin on his lips.

"What's so funny?" Hank asked.

"I used to hate this kind of work, but it kind of feels good now."

"Glad to hear it. Maybe you can take it on every day."

"I don't mind helping."

Hank gave his father a speculative look, but he said nothing else.

When they finished, Carl stretched his arms out. "I think I may have overdone it for my first day back at work."

"Probably, but you can have tomorrow off." Actually Hank didn't care if his father never finished the task, because it was such a relief to see him active again.

They heard the dinner bell ring before they reached the door of the barn. "Maggie's right on time," Carl said, looking at his watch.

"With Tim being sick and all… I thought we might have to make our own dinner," Hank said. But honestly, he was happy to have a warm meal ready for them.

"I should've stayed in and helped with Timmy. But it felt good to do some work. Son, I'm sorry for the way I've behaved this past year. I didn't realize what I was doing to myself or to you."

Hank paused and drew a deep breath. Blinking his eyes rapidly, he said, "I appreciate that, Dad, and I'm glad you've found your way back. I'm sorry I couldn't help you."

"It's not your fault, Hank. But every time I looked at you, I saw your mother in your blue eyes. It reminded me all over again what I'd lost."

"I'm sorry, Dad. I didn't realize that."

"I'm not sorry. I'm glad you have your mother's eyes. You'll always be a reminder of the happiness I shared with her."

The two men embraced, something they seldom did, before they continued toward the house.

Maggie stepped back from the window. She'd intended to turn a cold shoulder to Hank tonight, but she couldn't after watching the two men hug. With a sigh, she began putting dishes on the table.

Just as the men entered the house, the walkie-talkie crackled with sound, part of it a weak voice calling "Mommy."

"Dinner's on the table," she said hurriedly as she rushed to her son's side.

"I'm here, Timmy. What's wrong, honey?"

"My head hurts, Mommy," Timmy whispered as he laid his hot head against her.

"I know, baby. I'll get you some medicine. How does your tummy feel? Do you want to eat some dinner?"

"Can I have ice cream?" he whispered.

Maggie knew her son was playing up his sickness, but since he was still running a fever, she decided she would pamper him... just a little bit. "Yes, you can. Lie down again and I'll get your ice cream and medicine. By the way, did I tell you you're going to have a special guest tomorrow?"

"Who? Hank?"

"No, sweetie, not Hank. Aunt Kate!"

"Aunt Kate's coming to see me?"

"Yes, she is."

"When will she get here?"

"Tomorrow before lunch. Won't that be nice?"

"Yes, I love Aunt Kate!"

"Me, too. I'll be back in just a minute."

She jumped up and was surprised to discover Hank leaning against the doorjamb.

"Want me to stay with him for a few minutes?"

"That's not necessary," she snapped.

"Maybe not, but I'll enjoy it," he said and walked past her with a smile on his face for Timmy.

"Howdy, Tim. How are you feeling?"

Maggie hurried to the kitchen. She didn't want him with her son any longer than necessary.

When she returned five minutes later, her sick son was giggling, instead of complaining about a headache.

"Are you feeling better, Timmy?" she asked.

"Yeah, Hank told me a secret!" Timmy told her with a big grin.

"I see. Do I get to know the secret?" She

looked directly at Hank, sure he would tell her. But he shook his head no.

"Hank says ladies shouldn't know all the secrets," Timmy told her.

"Hank says a lot of things," Maggie returned, glaring at the big man. "We can manage now. You should go eat while the food is still warm."

"Yes, ma'am," Hank drawled and strolled out of the room.

"What is the big secret, Timmy?" Maggie asked once she was sure Hank was out of earshot.

"I can't tell you, Mommy. I promised Hank."

Maggie didn't press her small son further. She fed him the ice cream, after she had given him his medicine. They discussed Aunt Kate's impending visit until the ice cream was gone and his eyelids began to droop.

Chapter 5

When Maggie returned to the kitchen, she had every intention of cornering Hank and insisting he reveal the secret he'd imparted to her son.

But Hank wasn't there.

"Where's Hank?" she asked Carl.

"He went back out to the barn to see about something."

Maggie ground her teeth. "When will he be back?"

Carl looked up. "Something wrong?"

"Not really. Thank you for cleaning up after dinner."

"Hank said we should. Did you eat any dinner?"

"No, but I'll eat later. Then I think I'll do a little more baking. I want to have things ready when Kate gets here."

"Anything I can do?"

"No, thank you." Maggie began pulling out ingredients even as she looked out the window toward the barn every other minute.

After a while, Carl headed for his bedroom, pausing only to remind her to eat dinner. Maggie assured him she would. By eleven o'clock, she still hadn't eaten dinner. But she'd made brownies, cookies and two apple pies.

There was still no sign of Hank.

Maggie gave up and went to bed. She'd see him at breakfast the next morning. That's when she'd get things straightened out between them.

"Morning, Maggie," Hank said cheerfully.

"Sit down!" Maggie ordered.

Hank raised one eyebrow. "What's stuck in your craw?"

"I want to know the secret you told Timmy. I'm his mother. He's not supposed to keep secrets from me."

She stood there, his plate of food in her hands, and Hank suspected he wasn't going to get breakfast if he didn't tell her about the secret. "I can't do that."

He pulled out a chair and sat down, grateful she'd already poured him a cup of coffee. He took a long sip and waited for her response.

"Why?"

"Because it's a secret. We promised each other we wouldn't tell until it was time."

Maggie swallowed and then set the full plate in front of him, which made Hank revise his opinion of her. He'd recognized she was a good cook, a good woman, a good mother, but she was generous in defeat, too.

"When will that time be?"

"A couple of weeks."

"Do you promise it isn't anything that will hurt him?"

"Maggie, I would never do anything to hurt Timmy. He's a fine boy."

"All right. I don't like it, but as long as it doesn't hurt him, it's okay. But if I ever find out that this secret—"

"It won't hurt him," Hank promised. Then he dug into his food before she changed her mind.

After he finished eating, he stood and said, "I'm coming in for lunch today. I want to meet your Aunt Kate, since she's the person I thought I had hired."

"I was hoping I'd convinced you I could do the job," Maggie returned.

He thought she was teasing, but he wasn't sure. "I'm convinced, Maggie. But I'll be here to welcome Kate."

With those words he left the kitchen and headed outside to the barn.

Maggie watched him go. She wasn't sure she'd done the right thing. She still didn't think it was right for her little boy to have a secret from her. But she didn't want to force Timmy to break a promise just because she was jealous.

Maggie did recognize that jealousy was the reason for her anger. It didn't make her feel proud of herself. In fact, she was feeling pretty small. Maybe she'd clung to Timmy too much since his dad died.

Now that Kate was coming, perhaps she could ask the older woman for some advice. Maggie didn't want to ruin her child's life. On the other hand, she hated that Hank had been the one who'd pointed out her overprotective behaviour to her.

She hoped he didn't realize why she'd been upset.

After eating a good breakfast to make up for skipping dinner the night before, Maggie worked non-stop to make sure everything was just right for Kate's visit.

Carl volunteered to spend time with Timmy. His fever was down and the little boy was feeling better. Carl led him to the living room, a room seldom used. He settled the boy on the couch and sat down in the comfortable chair that faced the window. From his seat, Carl had a great view of the long driveway.

While the two of them watched for Aunt Kate, Carl plied his young friend with questions about his favorite aunt.

"Doesn't Kate have any children?"

"No. Her husband died a long time ago. I don't 'member exactly when."

"And she taught school?"

"Yes, but she's not teaching now. I was gonna go to her school, but she quit."

"Does she have boyfriends?"

"No, she's Aunt Kate," Timmy explained.

"How are you two doing?" Maggie asked, stepping into the room.

"We're watching for Aunt Kate, Mommy."

"That's good, but I think it may be a while

before she arrives. That's why I brought you some milk and cookies. I brought you some, too, Carl, only you get coffee."

"Thank you, Maggie. If your aunt is anything like you, I'm in love already."

Maggie felt an alarm go off. "Carl, Kate's just coming for a visit. She has her own life in Denver. She doesn't want to become a housekeeper."

Carl gave her a sharp look. "Maggie, I was just teasing."

He waited until Maggie had left and he and Timmy were enjoying the cookies.

"Is your Aunt Kate a city lady?"

"She lives in the city."

"Ah, right."

After their snack, Carl talked Timmy into returning to his bed for a little nap, just until his Aunt Kate arrived. Then Carl carried their tray back to the kitchen.

"All finished?" Maggie asked. Then she realized Timmy wasn't with Carl. "Where's Timmy?"

"I talked him into going back to bed for a little while. He was getting pretty tired."

"Oh, thank you, Carl. I appreciate you spending time with Timmy this morning. I want everything to look nice for Kate."

"Are you sure you don't want her to use the room down the hall? The one on the other side of me is a guest room."

"I appreciate the offer, but I want her to stay in my room. We'll do a lot of visiting while Timmy sleeps."

"Well, let us know if you change your mind. We don't want Kate thinking we're a bunch of hicks."

"She wouldn't think that, Carl. Not with this lovely updated kitchen."

"Linda had it remodeled right before she got sick. She was so happy with this new kitchen."

"I can imagine."

"Well, I don't want to keep you from your work. I'll go out to the barn and see if I can lend Hank a hand." He didn't really think Hank was hanging out in the barn. But he could see the driveway from there.

One of their cowboys was mucking out the stable and Carl thought about helping him. But he didn't want to smell like cow manure when he greeted Kate.

Not that he thought anything would come from Kate's visit. But he had to agree with his son. Kate looked perfect to him. That was why he was wearing his favorite shirt. And these days he was filling it out a little better.

Timmy awoke from his morning nap itching all over.

"Don't scratch, Tim. It will make scars," Maggie cautioned. But he ignored her and scratched wherever a blister had formed.

Maggie hurried him to the bathroom for a soothing oatmeal bath.

"But I took a bath last night," Timmy protested.

"I know, honey, but this will stop the itching. You'll see," she promised.

When she got him out of the bath, she made him stand still while she dotted every eruption on his skin with calamine lotion.

"I look like I have polka dots, Mommy. Aunt Kate will think I'm weird."

"No, she won't, Timmy. She knows what chicken pox is like."

"I think I hear her, Mommy. Aren't we finished yet?"

Maggie had thought she heard a car door a few minutes ago, but she couldn't be sure.

"Just a minute and I'll be through. Okay, that should do it. You can put on your underwear and a T-shirt. Here are your jeans."

She'd decided he should wear jeans since it was hard to scratch through the heavy denim.

"I think I hear Aunt Kate's voice. Help me, Mommy!"

Since Timmy was trying to walk as he put on his jeans, he was having difficulties. She stopped him and got his jeans zipped up and his T-shirt pulled down.

"Okay, you can go as far as the kitchen. Don't go on the porch without your shoes. And here are some socks, too."

"Aren't you coming, Mommy?" Timmy asked when he reached the bathroom door.

"I'll be out as soon as I clean up this mess," she answered, not really believing Kate had arrived. Besides, she wanted to get the bathroom sparkling clean since they'd be sharing it with Kate. She'd cleaned the room earlier, but some of her handiwork had been undone by her son's unexpected bath.

When she reached the kitchen a few minutes later, she looked out the window, just checking, and saw the car Kate drove. With a gasp, she raced out on the back porch, looking for Kate and Timmy. She found them both sitting with Carl on the back porch, visiting.

"Kate! Why didn't you let me know you

were here?" Maggie demanded as she hugged her only close relative.

"Timmy told me you were cleaning up in the bathroom. I thought maybe I should wait here until you were ready. Besides, Carl has been entertaining me."

Kate always found enjoyment wherever she was, and it seemed to be true now, as well.

"I had everything ready until Timmy's chicken pox erupted. I had to give him an oatmeal bath and put calamine lotion on him."

"We certainly noticed that, didn't we, Timmy boy?" Carl said with a smile.

"I'll put lunch on the table. Timmy, do you want to ring the bell for Hank? He said he was coming in for lunch to meet you, Kate. He thought he was hiring you when he hired me."

"I certainly bet he wasn't disappointed," Kate said, a big smile on her face.

Maggie could've told her he was so disappointed that he fired her on the spot, but thought better of it.

"Maggie's been great. She brought me back from death's door," Carl said.

"Good for her. It sounds like you'd had a

hard time of it, Carl. Losing someone you love is difficult."

"Yeah, Linda and I had been together thirty-six years. I couldn't seem to find my way alone."

"You were lucky to have that long a time together, but I understand how hard it can be."

"Maggie said your husband died young."

Kate nodded, not saying anything.

"Kate, you want to help me put out lunch?" Maggie asked, afraid to leave her to Carl's company. It might be a real downer.

"Of course, Maggie. I'm sorry, I should've offered."

Once the two ladies were inside, Maggie said, "I can manage, Kate. I was afraid Carl might be more than you could handle on your first day."

"Oh, no, I find him charming. I can see he's been ill, but he seems to be on the road to recovery."

"I think so. He's actually worked a while for the past two days. At least, I think he worked. He spent some time in the barn, which was a change for him."

"That's good. How old is he?"

"Why?" Maggie asked sharply.

"Just curious. If he was as bad as you said, it will take longer than a few weeks to get him back to good health."

"He's fifty-eight," Maggie said reluctantly. "I've seen pictures of him just before his wife died. He looks a lot younger in the pictures." She took chicken salad and fruit salad that she had prepared earlier that morning out of the fridge. "There's a pasta salad in there, too. Will you get it for me?"

"Of course," Kate agreed, getting up at once.

Meanwhile Maggie put some rolls in the oven before she poured the iced tea. By that time, Hank, Carl and Timmy came in.

"Have a seat, gentlemen," Maggie said as she put the iced tea at everyone's place except Timmy's. She poured him a glass of milk.

"Hank, this is my Aunt Kate. Kate, this is Hank Brownlee."

"Pleased to meet you, ma'am," Hank said, extending his hand.

Kate shook his hand. Then she sat down beside Carl, saying, "Like father, like son."

Carl beamed at her. "Thank you very much."

"Maggie, I can see why you're happy here," Kate added.

Carl continued to look happy. Hank, how-ever, frowned and Maggie was outraged.

"Don't let the rolls burn," Kate said.

Maggie opened the oven and took out the perfectly browned rolls. She dumped them into a breadbasket and put it on the table.

"Good call, Kate," Carl said.

Maggie ground her teeth together and said nothing. She joined everyone at the table, watching Timmy's choices. When he ignored the vegetable pasta, she added some to his plate and told him to eat it.

"Aunt Kate, do I have to?" he whined.

Maggie looked at Kate, holding her breath.

"Of course you do, Timmy. You always have to do what your mother tells you to do." She ignored Timmy's pout and talked to Carl.

Maggie took her son by the hand and led him to their bedroom. "Timmy, don't you ever do that again," she said sternly.

"What, Mommy?"

"Ask Aunt Kate to change what I have told you to do. I am your mother. I'm not going to tell you to do anything that will hurt you. And you put Aunt Kate in a bad position. You owe her an apology. Do you understand?"

"Yes, Mommy, but I don't like that pasta stuff."

"I don't care whether you like it or not. I said for you to eat it and that's what you have to do. Do you understand?"

"Yes, Mommy."

No one said anything when they returned to the table. Timmy waited until there was a pause in the conversation and said, "I'm sorry, Aunt Kate."

"It's all right, Timmy. But you know your Mommy loves you, don't you?"

"Yes," he agreed. Then he picked up his fork and pushed the pasta around his plate.

Maggie said nothing, but she kept an eye on her son. She didn't like the line drawn in the sand today on Kate's first visit, but she had no choice.

When Kate and Carl, along with Hank, finished their meal, they stood and started out of the kitchen. Timmy crumpled his napkin into his plate and slid from his seat.

"Timmy, sit back down, please." Maggie didn't even look at him. But she knew he obeyed her.

"But Mommy, I want to go with Carl when he shows Kate the barn," Timmy said.

"I'm sorry, sweetie, but you're sick. You need to go back to bed for another nap…after you finish your lunch."

"I'm not hungry anymore," he assured her with a smile.

"Nice try. Take the napkin out of your plate and eat your vegetable pasta like I told you to do." She began clearing the table, loading the dishwasher. There was plenty of all three salads left over. She covered them and put them in the fridge.

"Hurry up, Timmy. I have chores to do."

"It's okay, Mommy. I'll be all right."

"No, I'm not leaving you alone so you can throw the pasta in the trash." She pulled out a chair and sat down.

With a disgruntled look, Timmy picked up his fork and began eating the pasta. He took another drink of milk after every bite. After ten minutes, Maggie took his plate and put it in the dishwasher. "Thank you, Timmy."

"You're welcome, Mommy. Now can I go to the barn?"

"No, dear. The doctor said you need rest to get better. And besides, you look like you need another nap."

"Aw, Mommy," he complained, but Maggie could tell he didn't mean it. He headed to the bedroom too readily. She followed him, helping him out of his jeans and under the covers. She sat with him for a few minutes, but it didn't take long before he fell asleep.

She tiptoed out of the room, pulling the door closed behind her. She put in another load of clothes. Then she began folding the clothes in the dryer. She was just finishing that job when she heard the back door open. She came out of the laundry room with a stack of towels in time to greet Kate.

"Hi. Back from your tour?"

"Yes. I should've stayed and helped you clean up the kitchen."

"You're not here to work, Kate," Maggie said and smiled. "I just need to put these away."

"Maggie?" Kate called.

Maggie turned around. "Yes, Kate?"

"Carl said there's a guest room down the hall. I thought it might be easier on all of us if I slept in the guest room. I don't want to crowd you and Timmy, especially when he's sick."

Maggie forced her facial features to remain blank. Taking a deep breath, she said, "Of course, if you'll be more comfortable there." She turned around again. "I'll get it ready in just a few minutes."

"Maggie, I can—"

"No! It's my job, Kate." She never turned around. Instead, she put the towels in the guest bath and in Carl's bath, before going down the hall and quickly readying the guest room for Kate. Then she went to the kitchen where she found Kate and Carl. "Your room is ready, Kate. Where are your bags?"

"In the car. I'll go get them."

"Give me your keys. I'll get them," Maggie said, holding out her hand.

"Naw, Maggie," Carl protested, "you've got enough work. I can bring in Kate's bags. I'll show her the room and everything. You go take a break."

As the couple went out the door, she heard Timmy wake up, unhappy. She hurried into his room. After more calamine lotion, she convinced him to stay in bed and color pictures.

She returned to the kitchen to discover it was time to start supper. She went ahead and prepared the evening meal.

As she finished cooking Timmy called her, and she hurried to his side. When she returned to the kitchen, Kate and Carl were pouring the iced tea.

"Glad you got a chance to rest, Maggie," Carl said with a big smile. "We've poured the tea. Is there anything else for us to do?"

Chapter 6

Kate's visit wasn't going the way Maggie had imagined it. She'd pictured Kate and herself having several heart-to-heart talks where she poured out her problems and Kate reassured her she was doing just fine.

Instead, it appeared Carl was having those heart-to-heart discussions with Kate. He never left her side. Not that Kate was objecting. Maggie could hear her trill of laughter frequently while she worked.

By the third morning of Kate's visit, Maggie was exhausted. Timmy had awakened three or four times each night since Kate had arrived. She served Hank's breakfast at the usual time, but she could barely keep her eyes open.

"Maggie, are you all right?"

She jerked her eyes open and stared at him. "What?"

"You seem awfully tired. Are you staying up too late visiting with Kate?"

"No. Timmy has to have several baths during the night because of the itching."

"Go back to bed now. I'll put my dishes in the dishwasher when I'm finished."

"Thank you, but I need to do some laundry."

Hank leaned toward her and said sternly, "That's an order, Maggie, not a suggestion."

"But your dad—"

"I'll explain. Go to bed."

Maggie nodded and staggered into the bedroom where Timmy was sleeping. He'd just had a bath at five-thirty, so he should be good for three or four hours. Maggie crawled into bed and sank into sleep.

When Carl and Kate came into the kitchen at eight-thirty, Carl found a note left by his son.

"Hank says Maggie was up half the night

with Timmy, and he sent her back to bed. Looks like we're on our own for breakfast."

"That's not a problem. I love to cook, but I didn't want to horn in on Maggie's territory."

"I'm sure she wouldn't have felt that way. But feel free to cook now. I won't complain," Carl said with a laugh.

After cooking a fine breakfast, the two of them did the dishes and tidied the kitchen.

"What else can I do to help Maggie? How about laundry?"

Carl nodded. "Yes, she does laundry every day. We're getting pretty spoiled around here."

"Then I'll do laundry."

"And I'll make my bed," Carl promised.

Kate took a laundry basket first to her room, then to Carl's, where he was attempting to make his bed. She assisted him and then sent him off to the barn. After she'd gathered his laundry, she started down the hall.

The door to Hank's bedroom stood open and she couldn't help but notice the mess in his room. She decided Maggie must've been too busy with Timmy to do all her jobs lately. Kate entered his room and took out several loads of laundry. Then she came back and stripped his bed, which didn't look like it had been made in several weeks at least.

She found clean linens and made the bed. Then she ran the vacuum over the carpet and dusted the furniture. She thought the room looked much better after she'd finished.

Kate didn't say anything to Carl about what she'd done. She didn't want him thinking Maggie couldn't do her job. When she had the laundry going, she came back into the kitchen and whipped up a casserole for lunch, which, with a salad and hot rolls, would be enough to hold everyone until dinner.

She heard Timmy exhorting his mom to wake up and she hurried into their room. "Timmy, Mommy needs to sleep. Why don't you come to the kitchen and show me how well you're coloring now? Mommy said you stay in the lines really well. And I'll fix you some chocolate milk for breakfast."

Timmy was easily persuaded to leave his mother. He went to the kitchen in a T-shirt and shorts that Kate found for him to wear.

Once he was at the table coloring and drinking his chocolate milk, he asked, "Is Mommy sick? Does she have the chicken pox, too?"

"No, Timmy. She hasn't been getting

enough sleep with all the work she has to do and taking care of you. So we're giving her a vacation for the day. While you're coloring, I'll make us some chocolate pies for dessert tonight."

"Oh, goody, I love your chocolate pies," he assured her.

However, when Kate was halfway through making the pies, Timmy began to itch and scratch. He told Kate he needed his bath to stop the itching.

"Oh, honey, I can't do that right now. It would ruin the pies if I stopped in the middle of making them."

"Come on, Timmy, I can give you your bath," Maggie said from the door to the kitchen.

"Oh, Maggie, you're up. I hope you feel better."

"Yes, I do. Thank you. Are you making those for dessert tonight?"

"I thought it might help you out. Besides, you know how I love to cook." Kate smiled at her.

"Yes, thank you, Kate, it will help me out." She took Timmy's hand and led him to the bathroom where she gave him another oatmeal bath. Then she coated him with calamine lotion and talked him into using the game book in his room until lunch. She hurried to the kitchen to throw together a hasty lunch.

"I made a casserole for lunch," Kate assured her. "All we need to do is make a salad and cook some hot rolls."

"Thank you, Kate. I didn't intend for you to do all this work," Maggie said.

"I haven't done much, Maggie. I should've done more. I feel guilty because I got distracted by Carl's attention. It—it felt good."

Maggie's head snapped up. "You l-liked Carl's attention?"

"He's a charming man, and I've avoided single men for a number of years. But Carl is wonderful."

"I had no idea you'd be interested in any man," Maggie said slowly, studying Kate's red cheeks.

"You were too young to remember or know what I went through after Rodney's death. I tried dating, but since I was a widow, the men seemed to feel I should go to bed with them at once. I gave up and avoided dating altogether. Carl is—is a pleasant companion. I enjoy his company."

"Then I'm glad. Whatever happens, I'm glad you're risking it."

"Me, too. And you should think about doing the same. I intended to talk to you before you left, but everything happened so suddenly. You shouldn't waste the best years of your life being lonely."

"But I have Timmy to think about."

"Don't you think Timmy would benefit from having a daddy?"

"I'm not sure. Besides, Carl is spending time with Timmy."

"Doesn't Hank?"

"He has a lot to do."

Hank didn't come in for lunch, which proved Maggie's words to be right. After Timmy finished his lunch, Maggie took him back to their room and put him to bed. As tempted as she was to join him, Maggie went to the laundry room and found the washing machine loaded with clothes. As she transferred them to the dryer, she noticed a shirt Hank had worn several days before.

With a frown, she looked more closely at the other clothes. They all seemed to be Hank's. With a gasp, Maggie put them in the dryer. Then she ran down the hall to Hank's room. Just as she had feared, his room was meticulously neat with no dirty clothes on the floor.

It didn't take long to figure out that Kate had cleaned his room, thinking she was doing Maggie a favor. Maggie knew Hank wouldn't look at it that way. He'd forbidden her to enter his room.

There was nothing she could do about it now. Strewing his clothes about his room wouldn't convince him that his things hadn't been touched. She continued to do his laundry. When each load was finished, she folded his jeans and underwear and hung up the shirts. She didn't think he'd done laundry since she'd gotten there, which meant he must be running out of things to wear.

But she didn't expect praise for her efforts.

Kate had volunteered to cook dinner tonight, so Maggie did all the laundry and entertained Timmy for the rest of the afternoon. The extra sleep she'd gotten that morning, in addition to Kate's activities, made it possible for her to get all her chores done.

When they gathered for dinner, Hank came in and washed up on the porch. Then he sat down at the table without going to his room. The longer he didn't go to his room, the happier Maggie was.

After dinner, she sent Carl and Kate away, telling them she'd clean up the kitchen.

Carl suggested he and Kate take a ride and he could show her the area. Kate accepted Carl's offer.

Hank sat at the table, frowning as the other two left the kitchen. "What's going on?"

"What do you mean?" Maggie asked, though she thought she could guess.

"Dad and your Aunt Kate. Where are they going?"

"Carl said he wanted to show Kate the neighborhood."

"Hell! There's nothing out there but land."

"But there's a full moon tonight."

He frowned ferociously at her. "What does that have to do with anything?"

"Come on, Hank, you know what it has to do with a drive."

"Are you trying to cook something up between my dad and your aunt?"

Maggie turned and stared at him, putting her hands on her hips. "Isn't that what you had in mind when you thought you were hiring Kate?"

"Yeah, but I don't need her now."

"What do you mean?"

"You've fixed Dad up and he's happy now.

He doesn't need to marry some woman. He can remember Mom and that will be enough."

"Did you ask him if memories will be enough?"

"What are you hoping for? That he'll marry Kate and you'll be able to cash in on what she'll inherit?"

Maggie couldn't believe he'd said such a thing. "I don't have any intention of cashing in on anyone's inheritance."

"Well, you might warn your aunt. I don't intend to let things get out of hand. If she doesn't behave herself, I'll have her out of here in no time."

"I don't have to warn my aunt about anything."

"We'll see. You'd better enjoy her while she's here, because I don't think she'll be staying long."

Hank charged down the hall toward his bedroom, and Maggie held her breath. She certainly wouldn't tell him Kate had invaded his space. If she did he'd send her aunt packing.

"Maggie!" he shouted, anger in his voice.

"Yes, Hank?" She moved down the hall as if his summons had been a normal one.

"I thought I told you not to clean my room."

"You did, but I wanted you to know how much I appreciated your kindness this morning. I thought this," she said gesturing to his clean room, "would let you know I was grateful."

"It wasn't necessary, especially since I told you not to come in my room."

"If that's what you want, I won't do any more of your laundry or clean up your room or change your sheets."

"That's what I want. And let me know when Dad and Kate return."

"Why?" Maggie asked.

"Because I want to know. I need to discuss, uh, something with Dad."

Maggie didn't believe him. She thought he intended to warn his father about scheming women. But how could she convince Hank that Kate was good for Carl? Kate was not one of those kind of women, she thought.

"I will if I'm still up. I intend to get to bed early so getting up with Timmy won't wear me out." She didn't figure he could argue with those plans.

"Then, if you haven't told me they're back when you're ready for bed, let me know. I'll wait up for them."

"Oh! You're being ridiculous! Maybe you

should take a flashlight and drive around the area to see if you can find them enjoying a tryst in some secluded spot!"

"You're the one being ridiculous! They're too old to want to...never mind. Just let me know."

She nodded in agreement and headed back to the kitchen to finish cleaning up.

Half an hour later, she knocked on Hank's door. "Hank, I'm going to bed now."

There was no answer.

She knocked again and repeated what she'd said.

No answer.

After a moment, she turned the doorknob and peeked in. Hank was lying on his bed, still wearing his jeans, but he was sound asleep.

Maggie debated waking him up, but she figured he'd come to no harm sleeping in his jeans. If she woke him up, he might say something ugly about his father or her aunt. She quietly closed the door behind her and headed for her bedroom, hoping to get a few hours sleep before Timmy woke her up.

When Hank arrived at the breakfast table the next morning, he wasn't in a good mood. "I thought you were going to tell me when you went to bed."

"I did," Maggie said, putting his plate in front of him.

He continued to glare at her. "Then why don't I remember it?"

"Because you were already asleep."

"How do you know that?"

"I opened your door when I didn't get an answer. You were asleep on your bed."

"Why didn't you wake me up?" he growled.

"Because you were obviously tired."

"When did they get home?"

"I don't know," Maggie said, shrugging her shoulders.

"You act like you don't even care!" he snapped.

Maggie refilled his coffee cup and said, "Why should I? I don't think they're doing anything that will hurt anyone, including you."

"That's not up to you to decide, lady. But don't worry. I'll talk to Dad at lunch." Then he devoted his attention to his breakfast. When he finished, he left the house without a word.

When Carl and Kate came to the kitchen for breakfast, Maggie had it ready. Both of them told her how much they appreciated her hard work.

Then Kate said, "I made my bed, Carl's bed and Hank's, too. I thought that would save you some time."

"And I suppose you put his dirty clothes in the laundry along with yours and Carl's?" Maggie asked.

"Yes, I did. There was no reason for you to have to go to our rooms to pick things up since I was coming this way."

"Yeah, thanks. Did you enjoy seeing the neighborhood?"

Kate blushed, which told Maggie how they'd spent at least part of their time. "It was lovely."

Carl was beaming. "We had a great time. Kate likes the wide-open spaces."

"Yes, I'm sure she does. Um, Hank had something he wanted to talk to you about last night, but he fell asleep. He said he'd discuss whatever it was when he came in for lunch today."

"Good. I'll be here," Carl said cheerfully.

After they'd eaten, Carl suggested they spend their morning in the barn. Before they could leave, however, Maggie stopped them.

"Kate, Timmy wanted to show you something, if you have a minute."

"Of course. I assumed he was still asleep."

She followed Maggie into the bedroom where Timmy still slept. Maggie put a finger to her lips and led Kate into the bathroom, closing the door behind them.

"Kate, Hank's unhappy. He doesn't want his father to remarry...or be unfaithful to his mother's memory. I don't know where your relationship with Carl is going, but Hank's going to inform his father of his opinion when he comes in for lunch. I just thought you should be prepared."

Kate stared at her. "But Maggie, we've spent some time together and, I'll admit, there were a couple of kisses last night, but that's as far as things have gone. Surely he isn't...you don't think he believes we've done anything wrong?"

"I hope not. But I think he's going to suggest that you cut your visit short. I don't know if Carl's strong enough to fight him."

"Should I prepare Carl for what's going to happen at lunch?"

"That's up to you," Maggie said.

"Kate, I'm enjoying spending my days with you," Carl said with a smile. "I can't tell you how much your visit has meant to me."

"Carl, have you discussed how you feel with Hank?" Kate asked hesitantly.

"Why should I?"

"It's just that…that he indicated to Maggie that he's not happy to see you sh-showing interest in another woman. He wants you to remain faithful to your wife's memory."

"He wouldn't say anything like that. Maggie doesn't know what she's talking about."

"Carl, Maggie wouldn't say anything like that unless she was sure of it."

"Maybe she's just jealous because you're getting all the attention."

Kate stared at him. "You can't be serious!"

"I don't think you can be, either."

Kate stood. "I think I'll go back to the house."

"Fine!" Carl exclaimed, staring at her.

Kate hurried from the barn. She needed to talk to Maggie. Then she'd pack her bags and head back to Denver.

Hank came in for lunch, determined to figure out what was going on and to put a stop to it. He wasn't going to allow his father to throw his life away.

When he got to the house, he found his father sitting on the front porch, alone.

"Hi, Dad. Where's Kate?"

"Inside."

"Oh. I thought you two were spending all your time together."

"We were."

"What happened?"

"She tried to tell me you were upset and intended to put an end to our being together. I told her she was wrong. That you wouldn't do anything to ruin whatever happiness I could find."

"Dad—" Hank began.

"Lunch is served," Maggie said from the doorway.

Chapter 7

Maggie had talked Kate into staying for lunch. She hoped things would work out and Kate wouldn't feel she had to leave.

Kate was helping her put things on the table when the two men came in. Timmy jumped down from the table and ran to meet them.

"Hank! I haven't told!"

"Good, Timmy. I knew you could keep a secret," Hank said, rubbing Timmy's head.

Maggie pursed her lips, trying to ignore the exchange.

"What's for lunch?" Hank asked, as if he didn't have a care in the world.

Carl didn't appear as happy. Maggie wondered if his son had shared his feelings with his father.

The two men sat down and Timmy crawled back in his chair. Then Maggie and Kate joined them. They passed around the food without speaking.

After everyone had been served, Kate said, "I wanted to thank you for letting me come visit Maggie and Timmy. Now it will be their turn to come visit me."

Hank's head snapped up. "You make it sound like you're leaving."

"Yes, I'm leaving after lunch. I don't want to outstay my welcome," Kate said with a sweet smile directed toward Hank.

Carl scowled in her direction. "Kind of sudden, isn't it?"

Kate didn't respond. Maggie got up and poured more tea.

"You're okay with Kate leaving?" Hank asked, frowning.

"I'll miss her, of course, but I wouldn't want her to stay if she feels uncomfortable." Maggie looked at Hank, letting him know that it was all his fault.

"Do you think Hank's responsible for Kate's leaving?" Carl asked.

"Yes, I do," Maggie replied, keeping her gaze on her plate.

"Kate must've fed you the same malarkey she tried to feed me," Carl said. "But Hank would never try to stop me from enjoying life. He worked too hard the past year trying to bring me back to life."

Neither lady said anything.

Neither did Hank.

"Why is everybody mad?" Timmy asked quietly.

"Don't worry about it, sweetie. No one's mad at you." Maggie encouraged him to eat his lunch.

"Is Aunt Kate leaving?" Timmy asked.

"Yes, but she'll wait until you go down for your nap. She'll come tuck you in."

"Will you, Aunt Kate?"

"Of course I will, honey."

The rest of the meal was eaten in silence.

When he'd finished, Hank stood and thanked Maggie for the meal and bade Kate goodbye. Then he walked out of the house.

Carl stood, too. "I can't talk you out of leaving, Kate?"

"No, but I've had a lovely time, Carl."

"Will you come back?"

"I don't think that's a good idea. Maggie

and Timmy can come see me in Denver."
Kate ducked her head, not meeting his gaze.

"Then have a nice trip!" Carl ground out
and stomped out of the house.

"So, what just happened?" Kate asked.

"I think Carl let Hank know that you had
said he would object to you and Carl finding
happiness. Hank realized he didn't have to
say anything. So he kept his mouth shut and
watched things work out the way he wanted
them to. I'm sorry, Kate, I shouldn't have
said anything."

"No, I'm glad you did. I wouldn't want to
cause problems between Carl and his son. I
really liked Hank. But not now."

"I think he'll get over it if he's pushed,"
Maggie ventured.

"I won't be the one to push him. I'll miss
you and Timmy. And what was that about a
secret?"

"I was going to ask you about that. I don't
like Timmy having secrets from me, but it
made me realize I may have held him too
close since his father died. He's four now.
Hank promised me the secret wouldn't hurt
him."

"I hope it's true."

"I do, too," Maggie agreed with a sigh.

Kate nodded. "Timmy, are you ready for me to tuck you in?"

"Yes, but I don't want you to go," he said.

"I don't want to go, but I have to. You and Mommy will come see me soon. Okay?"

She swung him up into her arms and carried him to his and Maggie's bedroom. After she kissed him goodbye and tucked him in, she and Maggie went down the hall to get her luggage.

"I'm sorry you have to go," Maggie said. "It was nice while you were here."

"I enjoyed it, too, though I wasn't much help."

"Yes, you were. Of course, you did mess me up a little," Maggie said with a smile. At Kate's questioning look, Maggie said, "Hank didn't want me coming into his room or doing his laundry. I got in trouble every time you did it."

"You should've told me!" Kate exclaimed.

"It doesn't matter. If he wants to live like a pig, let him."

"How strange that he would want that. Most men are thrilled to have someone pick up after them and do all the chores."

"I know." Maggie hugged Kate before she

bent over to pick up a suitcase and an overnight bag. Kate grabbed the other bag.

"It's hard to believe you'll be in Denver for dinner. We seem a lot farther away."

"Promise you'll take time off and come see me?"

"I promise. If not before, I'll come for Thanksgiving."

"That would be great."

They walked outside to Kate's car. Maggie looked at the barn and saw Carl standing in the shadows watching them. But he didn't come out of the barn to say goodbye.

Maggie stood there waving goodbye until Kate's car disappeared in a cloud of dust. Then she turned and went back in the house, not looking in Carl's direction.

Hank had ridden out to check on a herd. When he got back to the barn, he had an hour to spare before dinner.

Striding into the barn, he found his father sitting on a bale of hay, just staring off into the distance.

"Dad? What are you doing? Isn't the rocker on the porch more comfortable?"

"I can't go there."

"Why not?" Hank asked, bending over. His father's voice didn't sound right.

"Because Kate and I sat on the porch lots of times, talking about…things. I'd feel lonesome if I sat there by myself."

"Come on, Dad, she wasn't here that long."

"Long enough for me to love her."

"What did you say?" Hank asked in outraged tones. "What about Mom?"

Carl looked up for the first time. "What about your mother?"

"Don't you think you should be faithful to her memory?"

"I will always love your mother, but in case you haven't noticed, she's dead. I've been so lonely. When Maggie and Tim came, it helped a lot. But when Kate came, I found a soul mate. We remembered the same things, had done the same things. For the first time since your mother died, I had a real reason for living."

"Dad, I don't think you need to—aren't memories enough?"

Carl stared at his son. "Kate was right, wasn't she? You were going to tell me to get rid of her."

"I just didn't think—I mean, if you marry, she could make off with everything you've worked for, and you'd still be alone. It was too big a risk."

"But who are you to decide? Look son, I love you, but there's no challenge on the ranch for me. I've seen what a good manager you are. We could set up a trust that would protect the land. Kate and I could travel. I could see the world, with her at my side. It would be wonderful!"

Hank hung his head, his hands on his hips. Finally, he looked at his father. "I was wrong, Dad, and I'm sorry I messed things up for you. You were finally doing so well, I thought I could keep you happy. I hadn't thought—Kate seems to be a nice lady. I hope you can patch things up."

Carl stood and hugged his son. "I love you, Hank. You're the best son any man could have. I'm waiting for you to marry and have a son. But I still have some life to live."

"I understand, Dad."

"I'm going to Denver in the morning, if I can get Maggie to give me Kate's address and phone number. I don't think it will be easy though, I think Maggie's not very happy with either of us."

"Yeah, probably not, but me more than you. I'll go see if I can pave the way." Hank drew a deep breath, threw his shoulders back and marched to the house, knowing he would be facing a hostile Maggie.

The kitchen was empty when Hank reached it, but the aroma of roast beef permeated the air. He took a deep breath. Then he went to the laundry room, but it was empty. He went down the hall and found his bed made and the dirty clothes missing.

What was wrong with Maggie? He'd told her not to come into his room. He was trying to maintain his distance, trying not to become too dependent on the woman. Women disappeared. He'd had friends whose wives had just walked away, leaving them depressed. Of course, some of his buddies deserved that kind of treatment, but that wasn't the point.

Hank had seen his father almost destroyed by his mother's death. He was not going to rely on a woman to make his world right.

Walking back down the hall, he knocked lightly on Maggie's bedroom door.

There was no answer.

He put his ear to the door, but he heard nothing. He knocked again, louder this time.

He heard movement and waited.

When the door opened, he saw Maggie, groggy with sleep, staring at him.

"Yes?"

"I want to talk with you."

"I'm not paid to talk, Hank. Dinner will be served in an hour." She tried to shut the door, but he put his leather-clad foot in the way.

"Come on, Maggie. I need to apologize."

"You did what you thought was right. Why are you apologizing?"

"Because I was wrong. Do we have to have this conversation in whispers? Can't we go sit down in the kitchen with a cup of coffee?"

"You mean you want me to make it easy for you?"

"Maggie, please."

"Fine, I'll put on a pot of coffee, but first I have to fix my hair."

"What's wrong with it?" he asked. Her long blond locks were flowing over her shoulders in a way that made Hank think of satin sheets and long nights. His body reacted immediately to her tousled appearance.

"I'll be there in a minute." She closed the door in his face.

When she came to the kitchen five minutes later, her hair was braided, neat and tidy.

She'd washed the sleep out of her eyes and she efficiently prepared a pot of coffee.

"I'll take some cookies, too, if you have any."

"They would ruin your appetite for dinner."

"Come on, Maggie, you're not talking to Timmy." He glared at her.

"No, I'm talking to a man who caused problems for my aunt and his father and then pretended that everything was well and he'd done nothing wrong." She stared at him, daring him to deny what she'd said.

He didn't. Instead, he ducked his head. "I know. And I'm sorry. I was afraid—Dad had just gotten over losing Mom. What if he fell in love again and went through the same thing? What if I lost him? It seemed so much simpler to keep him from risking his heart."

"You mean you were trying to keep him sitting on a shelf where you could enjoy him when you wanted and ignore him at other times?"

"I thought I was doing something good. You make it sound like I was being selfish," he growled.

She poured two cups of coffee and sat down at the table. Taking a sip of coffee gave her time to think. Then, not quite ready to forgive him, she said, "Kate is the one you should be apologizing to. She was enjoying herself for the first time in a long time."

"I know, but—why did she wait so long before she started looking? She's a good-looking woman. She could've found a man."

"So now it's her fault that she's available? It takes a long time to recover from the death of a loved one, if you ever do. She said she tried dating, but, because she was a widow, the men thought she should jump into bed with them. So she stopped."

"Sex is part of a relationship."

"Really? So every woman you date sleeps with you? And then what? You tell her thanks and go on your merry way?"

"Wait a minute!" Hank protested. "This isn't a discussion about me. We were talking about Kate!"

"I don't want to talk about Kate." Maggie got up from the table and checked on the roast. Then she began peeling potatoes, keeping her back to Hank.

After a minute, Hank stood and crossed to lean against the counter beside her. "Dad wants to go to Denver tomorrow and see

Kate. Will you give him her address and phone number?"

"Why should I? Haven't the two of you caused her enough grief?"

"Dad says he's in love with her."

Maggie turned to stare at him. "That's impossible. They only had a few days together."

"I don't know how Kate feels, but Dad said he found a soul mate."

"And you're okay with that? Because Kate said she wouldn't come between you and your dad."

"I didn't think she'd care about that as long as she got what she wanted."

Maggie glared at Hank. "Kate's not that kind of woman. Yes, she would like a companion, maybe even—even a lover, but she wouldn't take her happiness at the expense of someone else."

"Then she's a pretty rare woman," Hank spat out.

"Yes, she is, and you need to appreciate her! Especially if you expect me to give your dad her address and telephone number." She turned her back to him.

Carl entered the house at that moment. "Hi. Is dinner ready yet?" He kept his voice casual but he watched Maggie and Hank carefully.

"Dinner will be served in half an hour," Maggie said, without turning around.

Silence.

Finally, Carl said, "Uh, Maggie, I was thinking…about going to Denver tomorrow for a little while. You know, I haven't been off the ranch lately and I need some new clothes."

Maggie didn't respond.

Hank cleared his throat. "Maggie thinks we don't appreciate Kate. She's not sure she should give us her address and phone number."

"Maggie, I appreciate Kate. In fact, I love her and I want to spend the rest of my life with her."

Maggie turned around to look at Carl. He straightened his shoulders and smiled at her.

"Kate liked you, Carl. I don't know how much. But she won't come between you and Hank."

"Hank has given his blessing. I explained how I feel about Kate and he understands now. He was just trying to protect me."

"Well, you did almost die from a broken heart after Mom died," Hank pointed out dryly.

"That's true, son, but I feel happy to have been given a second chance for love."

Hank shook his head. "It's a big risk, Dad. I don't understand why people put themselves out there like that."

Carl frowned. "What are you saying? Is that why you haven't found anyone?"

Hank sidestepped his father's question. "I'm not ancient, Dad. I've still got time."

"But you're twenty-eight. You need to be building a family while you're young enough. Time will get away from you." Carl took a step toward his son. "I'm so sorry if my— my sickness caused you to give up on sharing your life with someone."

"Don't be silly, Dad. That's not why I— I've been busy. It's not easy managing a ranch this size."

"Do you need me to stay here and take some of the burden? I thought you liked running the ranch." Carl moved closer, concern on his face.

Hank patted his father's shoulder. "Everything's fine, Dad. And now that I understand how you feel about Kate, I'm fine with you, uh, you know, doing whatever it is you want."

"Thank you, son," Carl said, beaming at Hank.

Maggie turned her back to both of them. Hank had lied to his father. She could see it in his eyes. He was scared spitless, afraid if he loved anyone, she might die, leaving him as weak and helpless as his father had been.

She hadn't realized that before. She'd thought he was grieving for his mother, but it was more than that. Was that why he didn't want her to clean his room? He didn't want to depend on anyone?

He certainly depended on her for food. At least his phobia didn't go that far. She put the potatoes on to cook. Then she began cutting up vegetables for a salad.

"Uh, Maggie?" Carl said.

"Yes, Carl?" she asked, but she didn't turn around.

"Are you willing to give me Kate's number and address?"

Of course she would, but she wasn't willing to give in just yet. "I have to think about it, Carl. The two of you hurt Kate badly. I don't want her to suffer more than necessary."

"But, Maggie, I want to marry her. We can travel and see the world, and come back here for visits whenever she wants. Doesn't that sound wonderful?"

"Yes, if that's what she wants."

"Well, we won't know if we don't ask her," Carl said, and Maggie couldn't hold out any longer. "I'll call and ask her what she wants me to do."

Hank seemed perturbed by her reluctance. "I'm sure we could get her number off the Internet, Dad. We don't have to rely on Maggie."

"She said she'd call Kate. That's what I want. All I'm asking for is a chance to explain to Kate, to tell her what I'm hoping for. If she's not interested, then…then I'll come back here. And I promise, if she turns me down I won't fall apart like last time."

Maggie drew a deep breath. "Hank, if you'll finish the salad, I'll go call Kate."

Chapter 8

"Kate? It's Maggie. I wanted to be sure you got home safely."

There was a pause before Kate said, "I'm home safely. I should've called you, honey, but—I'll admit I'm a little depressed."

"I'm sorry," Maggie said. Then she looked up to see Carl standing in the doorway of her room, a questioning look on his face. "Uh, Kate, Carl was thinking of coming to Denver tomorrow and wondered if I could give him your number and address."

More silence. Then Kate said, "I don't think that would be a good idea, Maggie. I don't want to cause any problems between Carl and his son."

"You wouldn't be. Hank and his father have come to an agreement. Carl wants to explain things to you. Then if you don't want to see him, he said he'd understand."

"Why don't I just talk to him now?"

"I think he wants to explain in person."

"Is he standing there listening to you?"

"Yes," Maggie said in relief. She'd been uncomfortable talking to Kate with Carl listening in.

"Put him on the phone."

Maggie held the receiver out to Carl. "She wants to talk to you."

Carl froze. Then he moved toward her. "Are you sure?"

"Yes. Come on, Timmy. We need to finish supper."

Timmy slid off the bed where he'd been coloring. "Okay, Mommy, but I didn't get to talk to Aunt Kate."

"Another time, sweetie. Carl and Aunt Kate have something important to discuss." She led her son to the kitchen where she found Hank staring at various vegetables she'd intended to include in the salad.

He looked up in relief. "I'm glad you're back. Do you chop up the carrots?"

"You can. I like to grate my carrots," she said, taking the knife from his hand. "Just sit down and have some more coffee. You can talk to Timmy."

Those words caused Hank to realize his father hadn't come back into the kitchen. "Where's Dad?"

"He's talking to Kate."

Hank frowned.

"Hank, you do realize where your father is heading, don't you? If they marry, it's not going to shock you, is it?"

Hank drew a deep breath. "I'm willing to go along with what Dad wants. I was wrong to try to keep him from living. So, I'll—I'll deal with it."

Maggie shook her head and turned back to the salad. Then she took the potatoes off the stove, drained off the water, added butter and a little milk and whipped them until they were fluffy.

"Mmm, you make the best whipped potatoes I've ever eaten," Hank said. "Don't you think so, Timmy?"

"Yes, I love Mommy's potatoes."

"They'll be even better tonight because I'm

making gravy." She took the roast out of the oven. "Hank, could you slice the roast with the electric knife?"

"Sure," he agreed, getting up from the table.

"Here, Timmy, you can put a dab of butter on each roll before I put them in the oven."

"Thanks, Mommy. It's like we're a family, 'cause we're all working together."

Maggie stared first at Timmy and then Hank, who was wearing a shocked look. "Uh, no, honey. We're just all working together to get dinner on the table. Sometimes I need some help." And she concentrated on making the gravy.

When everything was on the table, Carl still hadn't come out of Maggie's bedroom. She thought she'd been making progress with Hank, but Timmy's innocent remark had wiped away any good feelings Hank had been having. From the look on his face, Maggie guessed he thought she'd been trying to trap him, which was ridiculous. She wasn't any more interested in making a family with Hank than he was. Even though he was handsome as sin…and adorable when he wasn't angry.

Maggie shook her head and brought her attention back on the dinner she was preparing before she got in trouble.

"Hank, I think you should go tell your father dinner is ready."

"I think we should start eating. He'll catch up," Hank responded, taking his place at the table.

Maggie gave a sigh of frustration. Finally, she walked out of the kitchen to her room. Stopping at the door, she said in a loud voice, "Carl, dinner is ready."

Carl looked up, waving to Maggie. She assumed he wanted her to do as Hank had suggested. But then he hung up the phone.

"Kate said she'd talk to me tomorrow. She gave me her address. She's going to fix lunch for the two of us."

"That's nice. Dinner's on the table."

Maggie turned and went back to the kitchen.

"What did Dad say?" Hank asked.

"He's coming." After several minutes, she said, "We might as well go ahead and serve ourselves."

"Yeah, 'cause it's a long way to your room."

"No, it's not, Hank," Timmy said, looking confused.

"I know it's not, buddy. I was just teasing your mom."

"Oh. I like that. There's Carl."

Carl had entered the kitchen, but he didn't seem to remember why he was there.

"Sit down, Dad, so we can ask the blessing and eat while the food is hot," Hank ordered.

"Oh, yes, of course," Carl said with a beatific smile.

"Look, Carl, I made a lake with my gravy," Timmy pointed out.

"Don't play with your food, Timmy," Maggie ordered.

"I don't think he's playing. That's how you eat potatoes and gravy," Hank said.

"Unless you're his lawyer, Hank, I think you need to stop interfering with how I raise my child," Maggie said. She realized she was overreacting. But the events of the day had been disturbing.

Hank narrowed his gaze and stared at her, but he didn't say anything.

Carl was smiling as he ate, not noticing anything going on around him.

Finally, Hank said, "What did Kate say?"

"Didn't I tell you? She's making lunch for us tomorrow." He went back to his dinner, as if his statement said it all.

"Did you tell her why you're coming?"

Carl stared at Hank. "I told her I wanted to explain what went wrong. I told her that she was right about your attitude, but that you'd changed it. You have, haven't you? Because Kate doesn't want you and me to be cross with each other."

"I'm fine with it, Dad. When are you leaving?"

"Tomorrow morning," Carl assured him.

"I know that, Dad. I mean are you leaving at eight?"

"Oh, no, probably before that. Are all my clothes clean, Maggie? I need to pack tonight."

"Why are you packing? Are you planning on moving in with Kate?" Hank demanded.

"Of course not. But we have a lot to talk about. I'll get a hotel room and stay a few days."

"I hope you'll let me know what's going on," Hank retorted with heavy sarcasm.

Carl didn't seem to notice. He excused himself to go pack, even though he hadn't finished his dinner, or had any of the chocolate pie Kate had made.

"Where's he going?" Hank demanded.

"He said he was going to pack," Maggie said calmly.

"Hell! He didn't even finish his meal. What's wrong with him?"

"I think he's in love," Maggie said, a smile on her lips.

"He just thinks he is!"

"You sure aren't acting like someone who accepts his father's decision," Maggie said with a superior look.

Hank came to breakfast the next morning in a bad mood. When Maggie greeted him, he growled. She guessed Hank was still upset with his father. She didn't think she'd done anything to upset him.

That was the end of any conversation until Carl wandered in with a large suitcase.

"Good morning," he said with a big smile.

Hank stared at him.

Maggie returned his greeting. "Sit down, Carl, and I'll fix you some breakfast."

"No, I have to go. I want to get an early start." He headed for the back door.

Hank could move swiftly for a big man. He got to the door before Carl. "Dad, sit down at the table and eat some breakfast! And that's an order! We don't want you fainting on the way to see Kate and having a wreck."

Carl looked alarmed. "Oh, no, that would delay me. Okay, I'll eat some breakfast."

Maggie put two pieces of bread in the toaster, fried some bacon and then two eggs. She watched in amazement as Carl began to bolt down his food.

"This is a very good breakfast, Maggie." Carl beamed at her.

Maggie knew he would've said the same thing if she'd served him cold cereal. Everything was wonderful in his world. She hoped Kate wouldn't break his heart. She'd already prayed that Carl wouldn't break Kate's. She wanted both of them to be happy.

"Oh, Hank, while I'm gone, you take care of Maggie and Timmy, okay? Keep them safe."

"Dad, we're not living in a jungle. They'll be fine."

"I know, but Timmy still has the chicken pox. He might need to see the doctor again."

"I'll take care of them," Hank finally said with a sigh.

"We'll be fine, Carl," Maggie assured him. "Give my love to Kate, please, and Timmy's, too."

"Oh, I will. I definitely will." That smile that told her he was thinking of Kate appeared on his face. She doubted that he even remembered what he'd just promised.

With his breakfast half-eaten, Carl got up to leave.

"Dad! You haven't finished your breakfast."

"I've had enough. I'll call," he promised and lifted the heavy suitcase.

Maggie wondered if he'd packed his entire wardrobe. She should've supervised his packing last night, but he didn't seem to want any help.

Even though he hadn't finished his breakfast, Hank jumped up from the table and took the heavy bag from his father, handling it easily. "I'll carry this to your truck."

"Thank you, son," Carl said. Then he hugged Maggie and kissed her cheek. "Bye, Maggie."

"Bye, Carl."

Maggie cleaned off Carl's dishes. She didn't know if Hank was coming back to finish his breakfast or not. If he did, it would be cold. She looked out the window. Hank was standing beside the truck, talking to Carl, who was behind the wheel.

Then Carl pulled away.

Hank started back toward the house.

Maggie grabbed his plate and put it in the microwave for a minute. When he came back to the table, his food was hot. She liked knowing that he ate good food. He needed it as much as his father. Of course, she was just doing her job, she told herself. It had nothing to do with Hank's good looks or his love and concern for his father. Of course it didn't.

"I hope you weren't trying to talk Carl out of going," she couldn't help saying.

Hank shot her an angry look. "That would be like trying to teach a tiger to roller-skate."

"He's very happy."

"He's very out of his mind. I'm hoping he remembers to stop for red lights. Whoever said love is blind sure knew what he was talking about."

"And that's a bad thing?" she couldn't resist asking.

"Yes. Being blind leads to trouble."

"Being alone leads to loneliness." She turned her back on him to clean up.

"Is that why you don't date?"

His personal question shocked her. She turned slowly to stare at him. "What makes you think I don't date?"

"I haven't seen any signs of it."

"I haven't been here much more than a month. It takes a while to get to know people. I intend to start going to church as soon as Timmy is over the chicken pox."

"So you dated in Denver?"

"Why all this interest in my personal life? I don't see you out dating anyone."

"I'm busy. This is a big ranch. I have a lot to do." He turned his attention to the food, as if their conversation was over.

"All work and no play," she murmured under her breath, determined to have the last word.

"Makes me a successful rancher," Hank said, shoving his chair back from the table. "I won't be in for lunch, but I'll be here for dinner. And I think I'd like some chocolate this evening."

"You're a chocoholic?" she asked in surprise.

"Yeah," he admitted with no shame. Then he donned his hat and headed for the barn.

Maggie poured a cup of coffee and sat down at the table. With Carl gone and Hank not coming in for lunch, her workload was reduced. How was she going to spend her day?

* * *

When Hank came in for dinner, everything seemed normal. He greeted Timmy, who seemed to be feeling better, and sat down at the table. "I'm starved."

"Coming right up. We're having stuffed pork chops," Maggie said with pride. The recipe took some extra preparation, but she'd had time today.

Hank frowned. "Stuffed with what?"

Maggie ignored his question. Instead, she put a plate in front of him with two stuffed pork chops. On the table were the potatoes he liked, green beans, hot rolls and a salad.

Hank picked up his knife and fork after he'd filled his plate and cut into a pork chop. After his first bite, he had no questions.

Timmy ate his entire dinner, too, without Maggie having to urge him. "Is it time yet, Mommy?"

"No, sweetie. It doesn't start until seven."

"What doesn't start until seven?" Hank asked.

"Monsters, Inc.," Timmy announced. "I saw the ad for it on television and Mommy said I could watch it." After checking on his mother out of the corner of his eye, he said to Hank, "But it will be hard to see it. Our television is really small."

"Timmy!" Maggie protested.

"What's the problem? Watch it in the family room. We have a big television in there."

"But you work in there in the evenings," Maggie said. "It would bother you, and it's not necessary. Our television is fine."

"How big is your television?"

Maggie frowned. "Thirteen inches."

"Let Timmy watch it in the family room," Hank ordered.

Maggie didn't say anything, but Timmy's eyes lit up.

"Thank you, Hank," Timmy said without prompting.

"No problem, buddy. Maybe I'll watch it with you."

"Good, 'cause I'm afraid I'll get scared," Timmy confessed.

"We'll keep each other safe," Hank said with a smile.

"So do you want your chocolate now or while you're watching television?"

"You really made something chocolate?" Hank asked, astonished.

"I work for you, Hank, and you did request chocolate when you left here this morning."

"Yeah, but—I'll have it now."

Maggie took down the cake plate and removed the lid. She'd made a chocolate cake with vanilla icing drizzled through the moist chocolate. Then she'd iced it with white icing topped by chocolate drizzle.

"That's a beautiful cake, Maggie. Right, Timmy?"

"Yeah, Mommy, it's great."

After she cut two pieces, a huge one for Hank and a more modest piece for Timmy, she poured both of them a glass of milk.

Hank looked up in surprise. "Milk for me?"

"It's good for you," she said and started clearing the table.

"Those pork chops were good, Maggie," he remembered to say as he took his first bite of cake. "Mmm, so is the cake."

"I'm glad you like it."

"Have we heard from Dad?"

"Not exactly," Maggie said, ducking her head.

"What does that mean?"

"When he hadn't called by two o'clock, I called Kate to make sure he got there safely. They were talking, lingering over the lunch Kate made."

"Had he checked into a hotel?"

"No, not yet." Suddenly she raised her head and stared at him. "Why? Are you planning on checking up on him?"

"He *is* my father, Maggie. And he hasn't been himself for a long time. I just think he should go slowly. He needs to get used to living again before he takes the barrel over Niagara Falls."

"You liken marriage to taking a barrel over Niagara Falls?"

"Yeah. They're quite similar. You can't see where you're going and you have no control over it. All you can do is hang on for dear life."

"Is that how your parents' marriage seemed to you?"

Hank finished his cake and stood up before he answered her. "No, my parents were very happy. They loved each other and—and they depended on each other. And that's the most dangerous thing of all. Because when one of you goes, the other is left with nothing."

"That's not true. Yes, it threw your father for a while, but he's got his footing again.

"And it's because he had such a wonderful marriage that he's willing to try again..."

"Maybe," Hank replied. Then he turned

to Timmy. "Okay, buddy, let's go watch that movie on the big television."

Hank took Timmy's hand and the two males left the kitchen together.

Maggie decided she needed to finish the kitchen quickly so she could supervise her son's evening. Half an hour later, with the kitchen all tidy, she hurried into the family room, a large, cheerful room that she loved. She discovered her son sitting in Hank's lap, both of their gazes fixed on the big screen.

Timmy noticed her at once. "Mommy! Come watch with us."

She tried to take the individual seat that matched the sofa, but Timmy protested, wanting her to sit beside him.

"Why don't you come sit in my lap?" Maggie suggested from the chair.

"Come on, Maggie," Hank said. "The show's starting again. I don't bite."

Maggie sat down on the couch, leaving a little room between her and the two males.

"Closer, Mommy, so I can hold your hand," Timmy urged.

Reluctantly, she moved closer, taking Timmy's hand in hers. But the proximity to Hank was disturbing.

As the movie wore on, she relaxed and

fought to keep her eyes from closing. She didn't notice when she lost the battle, but Hank did. Both mother and child fell asleep about the same time.

Timmy was asleep in Hank's arms. Maggie, on the other hand, was sleeping with her head straight back on the sofa. She looked very uncomfortable. Hank thought about waking her up, but the movie only had another half hour, and he was enjoying it. Instead, he stretched his arm out behind Maggie and pulled her closer so her head fell onto his shoulder.

When the credits rolled for the movie, Hank remained sitting on the couch, Timmy warm against his heart and Maggie's head on his shoulder. He breathed in deeply, catching the scent of her hair. He felt like a family man, without having to do the things necessary to create a family. Like fall in love.

Maggie stirred. Hank leaned over and kissed her on her temple. Then he wondered why he'd done such a thing.

"Uh, Maggie, the movie's over."

"Mmm, what?" Maggie asked, slowly opening her eyes. She lay there, looking at the television. Then she realized where her head was and jumped up from the sofa. "What—what happened?"

"You fell asleep. So did your child. I was the only one who finished watching the movie. It was fun."

"I—I'm sorry. We shouldn't have—if you'll give me Timmy, I'll take him to bed."

Hank stood with Timmy still in his arms. "I can carry him to bed. It's not far."

Maggie hurried ahead of him, as if he had a communicable disease. He watched her, her trim hips moving as she strode ahead of him.

When they reached the bedroom, Maggie turned down the covers and Hank laid the little boy down. "Where are his pajamas?" he whispered.

"He can sleep in his T-shirt and underwear tonight. Thank you for carrying him."

"No problem," Hank whispered. He was strangely reluctant to leave them, but Maggie stood there staring at him, waiting for him to leave.

"I'll see you in the morning," he whispered and tiptoed out of the room, feeling suddenly alone.

Chapter 9

It was four days before they heard from Carl again.

In the meantime, the atmosphere in the house was tense. It was as if they had all forgotten their roles. Every evening, Hank invited Timmy to watch the big television in the family room. And Maggie told him he couldn't.

She refused to let Timmy spend time alone with Hank. Yet she refused Hank's invitation to join him and the boy. And each night Hank lingered longer and longer over the dinner table. He and Timmy would talk about all kinds of things as he had a second cup of coffee.

When the call from Carl came, Hank was sitting at the dinner table, even though the meal had been completed for quite some time. He took the call in the kitchen.

"Hi, Dad. Good to hear from you."

Maggie's head snapped up. She stared at Hank.

"Oh? Yes, I guess so. I'm sure Maggie will agree." He paused and then said, "I'll be sure to tell her." He hung up the phone and returned to his place at the table. "Any more coffee?"

Maggie poured his coffee, waiting for him to speak.

Just when she thought she'd wring his neck, he said, "That was Dad."

"I figured that out, Hank. What did he say?"

"He and Kate are going to get married."

Maggie heaved a big sigh and sat down across from him. "Oh, my."

"I thought this would make you happy," Hank said, frowning.

"Yes, yes, it does."

"Mommy, what is it?" Timmy asked, looking from her to Hank and back again.

"Aunt Kate and Carl are going to get married."

"So Aunt Kate will live here with us? Yea!" Timmy clapped his hands, a big smile on his face.

"I don't know," Maggie responded. She looked at Hank. "What are their plans?"

"Dad wants them to get married here at the house. He said it could be simple, so you won't be overburdened, just a few people, but they'd like to have the ceremony on Saturday."

"This coming Saturday?" Maggie asked in astonishment.

"What's the problem?"

"I need to give the place a complete cleaning, and I need time to make a wedding cake, and cook food for the guests, and…"

"There's a lady in the neighborhood who makes wedding cakes. It's kind of short notice, but she'll do it for a higher fee. You'll need to make some, uh, finger food, but we won't serve a meal. We'll have it in the living room and serve the cake and food in the dining room."

"What about flowers?"

Hank didn't have an answer to that question. "What do we need flowers for?"

"Never mind. I'll call a florist I've used in Denver."

"Denver? That's three hours away."

"Yes, but Carl and Kate are there. They can pick up the flowers on their way here. When are they coming, by the way?"

"I think Saturday morning. Dad wanted the wedding at two in the afternoon."

"I'd better talk to Kate."

"Can I talk to Aunt Kate, too, Mommy?" Timmy asked.

"Yes, honey.

"You can congratulate Carl and tell Aunt Kate how happy you are for her."

"Why am I happy for her?" Timmy asked, a confused look on his face.

"Because she's getting married to Carl. He'll be your uncle, then."

"Do I call him Uncle Carl?" Timmy asked, making a funny face.

"I don't think so," Hank said. "I think you can keep on calling him Carl."

"Okay," Timmy agreed. "Doesn't he want to be my uncle?"

"No, it's not that. It's just…" Hank paused.

"It's just simpler to say Carl, sweetie. You know Carl likes you. He enjoyed sitting on the porch with you, didn't he?"

"Yeah," Timmy said with a grin. "We played cars and he told me about Hank when he was little. He was my size once, Mommy. Did you know that?"

"I guessed it, honey. Let's go see if there is a program that you might want to watch on television while I start getting things ready for the wedding."

"Okay," Timmy agreed eagerly.

Once she had Timmy settled, Maggie came back into the kitchen, only to find Hank still there.

"Did you want more cake, or some coffee?"

"No, but I thought you might need help."

"Yes, I do. I need to know where I can find a photographer."

"A photographer? We need one of those, too?"

"It's nice to have photographs of the ceremony, the happy couple. Is there a photographer in the area?"

"Larry plays around with cameras. He's pretty good, I guess."

"Can you call him? I need to talk to him." Maggie wondered if she was making a mistake in not seeking the services of a professional. Larry was very nice and all, but taking wedding photos was serious business and not a job for an amateur. If Larry wasn't any good...

"Sure. I'll call him right now."

"Thank you." She made sure there was still coffee in the pot.

When Hank hung up the phone, he said, "Larry's real excited. He'll be right up."

"Oh. Okay." She took a piece of paper and began making a list. She'd have to be organized to get everything done. "Oh, by the way, I'm going to clean your room again."

"But I told you I didn't want you in my room!"

Maggie stared at him. "I'm not going to have guests in the house and leave your room a pigsty. It would affect my reputation. So you'll just have to put up with dusted furniture, clean sheets and clothes hanging in your closet and not thrown on the floor."

A knock on the door announced Larry entering the kitchen. Maggie offered him a seat, a piece of cake and a cup of coffee.

He gladly accepted all three.

"What about me?" Hank immediately said.

Thinking he was talking about his room, she said, "I'll only clean it for a week."

"No, not that. How about a piece of cake for me?"

She stared at him, thinking about the huge piece he'd eaten just half an hour ago. "Well, yes, of course, Hank, if you want it."

"I do."

She cut two pieces of cake and brought them to the table. That's when she noticed that Larry was holding a photo album. "Oh, Larry, did you bring some samples of your work?"

"I thought you'd want to know that I know what I'm doing. I've never done a wedding before, but we can talk about the pictures you want. I won't charge for taking the pictures. All I need is enough money to cover the costs of the film and developing. This will be good advertisement for me."

"That's very generous of you, Larry. I'd be delighted to look at your work." Maggie reached out for the album, smiling at Larry.

"Yes, ma'am," he said, pushing the album across the table. He picked up his fork, but Maggie noticed he didn't actually take a bite. His eyes were glued to the album.

She opened the album, afraid of what she'd find. If his photography was amateurish, she intended to hire a real photographer.

The first photo was of a flower, its delicate bloom touched by dew. It was incredibly beautiful. She said nothing, turning the page, but hope was rising in her. The next photo was of an elderly cowboy, his hat clamped on his head as if it would never come off, deep wrinkles lining his face, but his blue eyes glinted with life.

She continued through the album, seeing Larry's artistic talent spring to life in each picture. Her heart was won over by the last photo. There stood Timmy playing cars on Carl's thigh, both of their gazes fixed on two small metal cars. Each face bore the same look of concentration.

"Your work is wonderful, Larry. How long have you been taking photos?"

"It seems like most of my life. But I only got a good camera a couple of years ago."

"I'll make a list of pictures we'll want. The main shots we'll need are of Kate and Carl, coming down the aisle, being married, tossing the bridal bouquet, cutting the cake. The rest would be up to you. We will cover your expenses and include an honorarium for you."

"No, really, that's not—"

"Eat your cake, Larry," Hank said, inter-rupting his protest. "Maggie's right. Dad and

I don't intend to spare expenses for this occasion."

"The wedding falls to the bride's family, Hank. I'll take care of the costs."

"No, I—"

"This sure is good cake, Maggie," Larry interrupted, his gaze shifting from Hank to Maggie and back again.

"Thank you, Larry. If you'll wait here, I'll get my checkbook so you can buy the necessary film."

After she left the room, Hank told his friend, "Whatever she writes you a check for, I'll duplicate it and you can tear up her check. Dad wouldn't want Maggie to try to pay for the wedding."

"Sure, Hank, but—"

"Just do what I say," Hank said sternly.

They both looked up as Maggie came back into the room. She handed Larry a check. "If this isn't enough, let me know, Larry. I'm so pleased that you're going to do the photos for Kate's wedding."

"I'm happy, too." Larry shot a look at Hank. Then he said, "This will be fine, Maggie."

"Won't you try the cake, Larry? Hank likes it."

"Oh, sure, Maggie." He took a bite and

closed his eyes as he chewed it. "Man, this is the best. Right, Hank?"

"Right."

The phone rang and Maggie jumped up to answer. "Brownlee Ranch."

Then she broke into a big smile. "Kate! I was going to call you. Wait a minute, I'm going to use the phone in the family room. Hank is in here with company."

She turned to Hank. "Will you hang up the phone in here for me when I pick up the other extension?"

"Sure."

Hank got up and took the phone from her. He greeted Kate and welcomed her into the family. Then he heard Maggie pick up the phone, so he told Kate goodbye.

"Are you okay with this?" Larry asked. "I mean, I know we talked about it, but sometimes you haven't seemed so happy about Maggie being here."

"Yeah, I'm okay with it now. It was a shock, but I guess it shouldn't have been. Anyway everything has worked out okay. And heck, I guess Maggie and me are practically family now. Besides, Kate and Maggie have a lot in common."

Larry looked surprised. "You're telling me

you've got a thing for Maggie like Carl has a thing for Kate?"

"No! Not at all. But she's—a good cook."

"Yeah," Larry agreed, a big smile on his face. "Is that the only thing that recommends her and Kate?"

"Don't push it, Larry!" Hank growled, looking away from his friend.

"Okay, okay. Are you all right about the pictures?"

"Sure. I knew you were good. That was a cute picture of Dad and Timmy."

"Yeah. You want a copy of it?" Larry offered, pride in his voice.

"I do. Include that in the price of the pictures. How much did she write the check for?"

Larry told him the amount.

"I'll bring you a check down in the morning. Be sure and tear that one up."

Larry shoved the check across the table. "Why don't you tear it up? I'll feel better about it."

"Okay, fine," Hank agreed, folding the check and putting it in his shirt pocket. "Eat your cake. You'll upset Maggie if you don't."

"Is that why you ate yours?"

Hank grinned. "You know I love choco-late."

"I know." Larry began eating his cake again. "Man, I've got to come back here to eat. She is definitely a great cook."

"Yeah. She's pretty good at everything. She's even a good mother. Just a little bit too good."

"What do you mean?"

"She babies that boy way too much."

"She won't let him grow up?"

"No. But I'm helping him," Hank said with a nod.

"What do you mean? You're doing some-thing his mom doesn't want? Hank, I don't think that's a good idea."

"Yes, it is. It isn't anything that will hurt him."

Larry took his last bite of cake. Then he stood and carried his dirty plate and cup to the sink. "Tell Maggie I loved the cake and I'll get ready for the wedding."

"Why don't you tell her yourself?" Hank suggested, frowning at his friend.

"I don't want to get involved in a fight be-tween you and Maggie."

Hank stood. "We're not going to fight. She doesn't even know about it yet."

"Hank, wake up and smell the coffee. You come between a mother and her young one and you'll have a fight on your hands. You know how those mama cows are when you want to take their calves."

"But she's not—"

"Are you leaving already, Larry?" Maggie asked as she came back to the kitchen.

"Yeah. I told Hank to tell you I loved the cake. I think I need to come back to dinner when you can stand me," he added with a grin.

"Any night, Larry. There's always plenty of food."

"Great. May I come tomorrow night?"

"Of course. We can talk more about arrangements for the wedding."

"Great. I'll see you tomorrow, then."

Larry hurried out the door with a wave.

"Did you upset Larry?" Maggie asked.

"Nope. He worries about the other boys getting jealous when he spends too much time here."

"And that's why he's coming for dinner tomorrow night?" Maggie asked, skepticism in her voice.

Hank shrugged his shoulders. "What did Kate have to say?"

"She said she wanted me to stand up with her, and your father wants you to stand up with him. They decided Timmy could be the ring bearer. And your dad asked if you'd called the wedding-cake lady yet."

"Not yet." He stood and grabbed the phone. It took some bargaining and a promise of a bonus, but Carl and Kate would have a wedding cake that would feed one hundred people. The cake would be delivered Saturday morning.

After Hank hung up the phone and turned around, Maggie asked, "A hundred people?"

"That's a guess. You know, when you have a celebration, your neighbors show up. I'll call a few of them tomorrow and ask them to call everyone else."

"So finger foods for a hundred people? Oh, and did you ask for a groom's cake?"

"Yeah, it's part of the package."

"Oh. Well, thanks for arranging that. If you'll let me know how much, I'll—"

"No, you won't. Dad asked me to make arrangements for the cakes. That means I pay for them." He turned to leave the kitchen.

"Wait a minute, Hank. We need to settle this. The bride's family is responsible for the wedding. The groom's family pays for the honeymoon."

"You think Dad and I are going to let you use your savings to pay for him to marry Kate? Not going to happen, Maggie, and you might as well get used to it."

"Hank Brownlee, you are wrong! Kate has some money. She's insisting on paying for the flowers. So, between us, we can handle this."

"You're doing the cooking. That's enough."

"Listen to me!" Maggie exclaimed. "This is the way we're doing it. Kate and I are paying for the wedding."

"I'll tell you what. I'll go ahead and pay for the cakes and you can take it up with my dad. After all, it's not my wedding."

"No, it's not!"

"What do I need to wear? Are we going formal? Or just a suit?"

"Just a suit and tie. You do have that, don't you?"

"Of course, I do. We aren't barbarians."

"I didn't mean to imply that you were. Do I need to take it to the cleaners?"

"Nope. I sent it to the cleaners a couple of months ago and I haven't worn it since. Do you have something to wear?"

"I think so."

"I can take you shopping, if you need to go. Larry can stay with Tim. By the way, will Tim be healthy by the wedding?"

"Yes, he's not communicable now, but his scabs should be gone by Saturday."

Hank stood there a minute longer, but Maggie said nothing else. "I guess I'll, um, go on to bed."

"Yes. I'll see you at breakfast," she agreed. She grabbed his cup and plate, which reminded Hank that Larry had taken his own dishes to the sink. "Uh, sorry, I could've... I forgot."

"It's all right. It's my job."

"Yeah, uh, good night, Maggie. That was a good meal tonight."

"Thank you."

"I'll just go say good-night to Tim."

"He may have fallen asleep," Maggie said, stepping closer to her bedroom. "He didn't get a nap today."

"I won't wake him if he's already asleep."

His words didn't reassure Maggie. She followed him to her room, rising on tiptoes to see over his shoulders. Unfortunately, he was too tall. She stepped into the room behind him to discover what she had expected. Timmy had lain down on the bed they shared and pulled the covers around him to watch television. He was sound asleep.

Hank stood there by the bed, staring down at the little boy. "He's a cute little guy," he whispered.

"Yes, he is," she whispered in return.

He turned to leave the room and Maggie followed him.

"Are you going to tuck me in, too?" Hank asked.

Maggie came to an abrupt halt. "No, I was going to finish cleaning the kitchen."

"So why did you come after me? I promised I wouldn't wake him if he was asleep."

"I wanted to be sure. If he awakened suddenly, he might be scared." She raised her chin and stared at him, daring him to say differently.

"I think you're too protective," Hank said.

"You have no right to say how I treat my child as long as I'm not abusing him," Maggie said, her voice tight.

"Maggie, I'm not trying to boss you about Timmy. I'm just trying to help."

"Well, you're not! I'll take care of my son without your help."

"You're making too much of a simple comment, Maggie," he protested.

"Good night, Hank," Maggie said, turning her back on him.

"Good night," he muttered as he walked down the hall to his room. He thought Larry had been right about a fight with Maggie. It was long overdue.

Chapter 10

The rest of the week was hectic. Maggie cleaned the house until every inch was spotless—including Hank's room. Each evening, she planned the menu for the wedding. On Friday morning she pulled the last load of laundry out of the dryer and began folding and hanging it up.

Then she noticed little pieces of paper. She picked the paper out of the laundry and suddenly realized what she'd found. Her check to Larry.

She knew she'd checked Hank's jeans pockets, but the check must've been in one of the shirts. Recognizing the shirt Hank had worn the night Larry had come to show her his photographs, she felt sure she'd found the source of the paper.

But why did Hank have the check?

Then it struck her. Hank was continuing to deny her her right to pay for the wedding. The tension that she'd felt all week escalated and she tore out of the house and headed for the barn, hoping Hank was still there.

She burst into the barn. "Hank!" she screamed.

Her voice echoed against the walls.

Larry came around the corner. "Maggie? Is something wrong?"

"Larry, did you cash the check I gave you?"

"Uh, sure," Larry responded, dropping his gaze.

"Then why did I find pieces of it in the laundry?" She crossed her arms over her chest and stared at him, waiting.

"Uh, I'm sorry, but Hank told me... I didn't want him to fire me."

"You know he wouldn't fire you, Larry. What's going on?"

Larry sighed and knocked his cowboy hat to the back of his head. "Maggie, Hank and his dad have a lot of pride. They want to pay for the wedding. You're going to have to talk to them."

"So Hank said what? Tear up the check and he'd pay you?"

"Yeah."

Maggie stood, staring at the hay-strewn floor. Finally she looked up and smiled at Larry. "Sorry I yelled at you."

"Seems to me you yelled out Hank's name. Not mine."

"True. Thanks, Larry."

Maggie did a slow walk back to the house. Larry was right. Her battle was with Hank and Carl, and she needed to talk to Kate about it. But not now. There was too much to do with the wedding preparations. But after some of that work was out of the way....

Hank headed into the small town nearest to the ranch. He was on his way to pick up an order of champagne for the wedding.

He figured he'd done all that was required of him. At least until tomorrow. Then he'd have to help his father dive back into the pool of life, risking heartbreak again.

Hank sighed. He'd promised to be happy for his father, but it was a struggle. Not that he didn't like Kate. What was there not to like? She was so much like Maggie: warm, loving, patient. His dad had picked a good one.

But life had no guarantees.

He parked his truck and got out. In the store, several people greeted him.

"Hank, big day tomorrow, right?" a neighbor called out.

"Right, Ben. A big day. Is my order ready?"

"Best news I've heard in a while," the owner of the shop said. "I thought Carl was going to just fade away."

"Yeah, me, too. Do you have the champagne, Kevin?"

"Sure do. All boxed up. Going to be a fine wedding. Do you need a recipe for a non-alcoholic punch? You know, for those who don't drink alcohol."

Hank frowned. "I hadn't thought about that."

"That's how lots of people do it. Champagne and then an alternative."

"Yeah," Ben agreed. "My wife's pregnant again. She can't drink alcohol."

"Congratulations, Ben. I hadn't heard."

"Yeah, we haven't told a lot of people. But we're real excited. You should try getting married and starting a family, too. It's a wonderful thing."

Hank noted the look on Ben's face. It resembled the look Carl had been wearing when he'd left the ranch to visit Kate. Love had struck again.

"I don't think I'm cut out to be a family man," he said as he took a credit card out of his pocket to pay for the champagne. Kevin handed him a piece of paper.

"What's this?" Hank asked.

"The recipe for my special punch," Kevin said and winked. "I only give it to my best customers. It's simple. Even you can do it, Hank."

"Thanks. We'll see you tomorrow."

After loading the champagne in the back of his truck, Hank stared at the paper Kevin had given him. He was right. It wasn't hard. He'd stop by a grocery store and pick up the ingredients.

Then Maggie could make it.

"Hey, Hank!" Ben called out. "I forgot to ask. Does your housekeeper need any help?"

"Why? Do you know someone I could hire?"

"No, that's not the way we do things. My wife could pitch in. She's a real good cook.

Tell your housekeeper to call Melanie if she needs anything."

"I'll tell her."

After Ben had driven away, Hank realized he might have another problem. Maggie was going to be introduced to their neighbors as the housekeeper.

And his father would be leaving to go on his honeymoon. How long did honeymoons last these days? And what would his neighbors have to say about him and Maggie living in the house alone?

Would his neighbors be suspicious about Maggie? Would they think he'd hidden her from them for several months?

He hadn't done that. Had he?

His neighbors would talk about them being alone. Maggie might get upset and leave.

She couldn't do that. He was helping Timmy. And—and he'd miss her.

Hank drove home without seeing friends waving goodbye to him. All he could think about was Maggie and Timmy leaving.

When Hank pulled into the yard at the ranch, he found Tim on the back porch.

"Hey, are you well or what?" he called.

"Almost. Mommy said I could play with

my cars out here for a little while. Hank, how long do I have to keep the secret?"

Hank hurried to the porch. "Quiet, buddy. We don't want your mom to hear. Remember?"

"She's busy making little pies."

"Little pies?" Hank asked, frowning.

"Mommy called them something funny, but they look like pies."

"Okay. I've got to carry in some groceries and things. I'll check on her."

Hank took the box of champagne into the house. In the kitchen, he found Maggie was working on little pies, just like Timmy had said. "Small pies? Will we need that with the cakes?" he asked.

Maggie looked up in surprise. "These are quiches, not pies. They're part of the finger foods."

"Oh, great. Here are the bottles of champagne."

"Oh, my. You're certainly going first-class." She continued to work on the quiches.

"I've got some groceries to bring in. I'll be right back."

"Okay," she said, not looking up.

Hank unloaded the truck and brought in the groceries.

"What's that?" Maggie asked as he set down two boxes.

"Uh, Maggie, we need a non-alcoholic punch for the wedding. Kevin gave me this recipe. He said it was easy."

Maggie put a tray of quiches into the oven before she turned to look at Hank. "A punch?"

"Yeah. Like, Ben's wife is pregnant. She can't drink alcohol. Neither can Timmy."

"Couldn't we just have some soft drinks on hand?" she asked, staring at the recipe.

"Is it too hard?"

"No, it's not too hard, but what am I going to use to serve it? And where am I going to store it after I make it?"

"You can use the refrigerator in the bunk house. And Mom had these big jars she made punch in. I'll get them for you."

He found the jars in the storeroom and carried them to the kitchen.

"Here they are. I'll clean them out for you," Hank offered.

"That's all right. I can do it. After all, you're paying for everything, right?"

Hank turned around slowly. "What are you talking about?"

"I found little bits of paper in the laundry.

I put together enough of it to discover the check I wrote to Larry."

Without thinking, Hank slapped the left side of his chest. Then his cheeks turned bright red. "I forgot to take it out of my shirt pocket and tear it up."

"So I gathered. I'm not going to argue with you about it. I'll take it up with Kate and Carl."

"Good. So I'll help out by rinsing out these jugs while you finish what you're doing," Hank said and began his task.

Maggie stared at him, frowning, until the buzzer went off on the oven. She opened the door and drew out a cookie sheet filled with small quiches.

"They cook that fast?" Hank asked in surprise.

"No, Hank. I already had this tray in the oven. The other one won't be ready for…" she paused to check her watch "…another fifteen minutes." Then she reset the timer.

They worked in silence for a few minutes. Then he said, "Uh, Ben's wife, the pregnant one, offered help, if you need it." He cleared his throat. "I, uh, have the number if you want it."

"What's her name?"

"Melanie. She's nice."

Maggie turned to face Hank. "Do you think she might be willing to serve cake tomorrow? And maybe she has a couple of friends who could help, too?"

"Well, sure. She's a good neighbor." He stopped what he was doing and dried his hands. Then he wrote the number on a piece of paper. "Just give her a call."

Maggie took the number and dialed it on the phone. Though she was tense when she first called, Melanie made things easy for her. She promised to serve the cake and round up a couple of other women to help out.

Maggie hung up the phone with a big sigh.

"Were you worried about that, Maggie?" Hank asked.

"Yes, I was. I didn't see how I could do everything myself." She tucked a stray lock of hair into her ponytail and seemed to gather herself.

"I could've helped if you'd told me what was wrong," Hank pointed out.

"I didn't know if you had any friends, other than men. You don't exactly socialize, do you?"

"Not in the past year, but everyone knew why. They all came after Mom died and brought lots and lots of food. But they all had their own places to run, and they figured I could take care of Dad."

"And you did," Maggie hurriedly said.

"No, I didn't. You did, Maggie. You and Timmy. I'll admit it stuck in my craw that Dad would respond to you and not me, but I'm over that. You did good, and I owe you."

"No, you don't, Hank. You pay me a salary to do what I've done. I think Carl was tired of—of not living, but he didn't have the strength to change. A little comfort food made the difference."

"Yeah, I'm not much of a cook."

"But you do other things well, Hank. You took care of the ranch. Without you, it would've fallen apart."

Hank gave her a rueful smile. "We're a great mutual admiration society, aren't we, Maggie?"

"Yes, I guess we are. But I knew you hadn't had time to mourn your mother. I'll admit you irritated me, but I tried to remember that you needed to deal with the loss."

"You were more patient with me than I deserved."

They smiled at each other, suddenly at peace...until Timmy came in.

"Mommy, I get to tell you my secret soon. Hank said."

Any soft feelings Maggie had for Hank disappeared. "Timmy, I think you should tell me about your secret now."

Timmy looked at Hank, pleading in every ounce of his being.

"Sure, buddy, you can tell her now, if you want."

Timmy was practically jumping up and down. "I'm going to get to sleep in Hank's little-boy room, Mommy. And in case I don't like being alone, I get to have a puppy to sleep with me!"

Maggie's horrified gaze swung from Timmy to Hank. She was speechless that he had promised such a thing without talking to her first. "Timmy, I don't think—"

"Please, Mommy?" Timmy begged.

"Maggie, you need to think about this before you make a mistake," Hank said at the same time.

"I beg your pardon? You want me to stop and think? Why didn't you? Timmy, go to our room and watch television," she ordered sternly.

"But Mommy—"

"Timmy, do as I said!"

As soon as the little boy had left the kitchen, Hank said, "Don't take your anger out on the little guy. Blame me."

"Oh, believe me, I do! How could you make such a promise without first asking me? I'm his mother!"

"Yes, you are, but you're holding him too close," Hank said in a reasonable voice.

"And you know because you've raised so many children? You're a bachelor, for heaven's sake! You don't know anything about raising kids!"

"I know little boys need to grow independent of their mothers. How long is he going to share a bed with his mother? He's not a baby anymore."

"Go away! I don't want to see you!" Maggie exclaimed. What made her anger even greater was the niggling doubt that he might be right. But Timmy was her son! She should be the one to make those decisions.

Hank stalked to the barn, scowling at the world.

"What's up, boss?" Larry asked from the tack room where he was repairing some equipment.

"I just got thrown out of my own house!"

"Who—uh-oh. You and Maggie had that fight, didn't you?" Larry was shaking his head.

"She's unreasonable! She won't even listen to what I had to say."

"I warned you," Larry said with a smile.

"Great! Now I've got my best friend saying 'I told you so,'" Hank said, and groaned.

"Well, I did," Larry repeated.

"That doesn't help me! It really is for Timmy's good. He's a great little guy, but she's turning him into a mama's boy."

"Well, at least you tried. I'm sure Timmy will remember that."

"Maybe I can give him a dog, even if it has to stay in the barn. But a boy needs a dog."

"Yeah. I remember your first dog. Used to follow you to the bus stop."

"Yeah. Old Buster was a great friend." Hank chuckled. "This puppy, the one I picked out, is Buster's grandson. He'll be a good friend to Timmy."

"If you can get his mother's consent."

"Don't have to if he's going to live in the barn. We don't have to tell her anything." Hank clamped his lips shut.

"Hank! Haven't you learned from your mistakes yet? You don't make arrangements with a little boy without consulting his parent. And that means Maggie."

"I don't see why—Okay, okay, I do see why. But—"

"What if it was your son and someone else made plans for him? Plans that would change his life?"

"I'd be grateful for their concern!"

"Like hell you would. You're protective of everything you own. You'd be even more so about your kids. You'd be like a mama bear whose cubs were being threatened."

"You don't know that, Larry! I can be reasonable!" Hank began pacing back and forth, running his fingers through his hair.

"Yeah, like you are now," Larry muttered.

Hank glared at his friend, but he gave up an argument he wasn't going to win. Larry knew him too well. "I'm going to the church to pick up the punch bowl and the cups. Want to come with me?"

"I'd better. You might start throwing things if I don't."

"Mommy?" Timmy said, peeking around the corner into the kitchen.

"Yes?" Maggie asked, her voice still stern with anger.

"I didn't mean to make you mad," he said, fear in his voice.

Maggie gave herself a mental shake. "Honey, I'm not mad at you. I'm mad at Hank. He shouldn't have—" She brought herself up short. She shouldn't place the burden on her son. "Never mind, honey. I'm not mad."

"Oh, goody. Then I can move into Hank's old room and have my puppy?" His face was flushed with pleasure, his eyes, so like his father's were sparkling.

"No, I didn't—I don't know. We'll discuss it after the wedding, Timmy. I have too much on my mind to think clearly right now."

"Okay, Mommy," Timmy said agreeably. He edged his way into the kitchen, as if he didn't quite believe she wasn't angry. Sliding into a chair at the table, he said, "The puppy is so little and soft. And his granddaddy was Hank's dog."

"Timmy, I don't want to discuss the puppy now. I have to concentrate on making the punch for tomorrow. Here, taste this and see if you like it." She poured a small glass of red punch for him.

He tasted it. "I like it, Mommy. It's better than Kool-Aid because it's all fizzy."

"Oh, good."

"Will it still be fizzy tomorrow?"

"Yes, honey. I won't put in the ginger ale until the last minute. It will be fine. I just had to see how it would taste."

"It's good."

"I'm glad to hear it," she said with a smile. Her mind was already moving on to the next item on her list.

"I bet my puppy would like it, too," Timmy said, shooting a look at his mother.

Maggie paused, took a deep breath and said, "I don't think punch is good for puppies. We don't feed puppies human food."

"Okay, I won't. Do you know what I named my puppy?"

Maggie wanted to remind him that he didn't have a puppy yet, but she couldn't resist the eagerness in his face. "What did you name the puppy?"

"Wiggles, because he wiggles a lot!" Timmy said, laughing out loud.

"That's nice."

"Hank said it was, uh, 'propriate."

"Yes, I'm sure he did."

The rest of her day was filled with stories about Wiggles and what Hank had said and the plans Timmy had made for his new little friend and himself. And Hank, of course.

After a steady diet of Timmy's conversation, she wanted to scream. Or slap Hank Brownlee!

Chapter 11

The next morning, Maggie showered early and curled her hair. Then she began organizing the kitchen for the day.

When she looked out the kitchen window and saw a truck with four men arrive, she couldn't imagine what was going on. They began unloading their truck, and she went to find Hank, who had yet to put in an appearance. "Hank? Hank! There are some men here unloading something from their truck."

Hank came out of his bedroom in boots, jeans and a T-shirt. "Thanks, Maggie. Can you put on a pot of coffee?"

He kept moving, and he hadn't answered her question.

"But, Hank, what are they doing?"

Since she'd already made coffee, she returned to her kitchen and made a few sausage rolls to go with the coffee. At the same time she was making the rolls, she made a couple of quick trips to the living room to see what the men were doing.

When a green-striped awning was set up on the front lawn, she nodded in agreement. Of course. They couldn't fit a hundred people in the house. A tent with tables and chairs was the perfect idea.

Maggie loaded a tray with the pot of coffee, five mugs—since Hank had been helping them—and a plate of sausage rolls and carried it to one of the tables under the awning.

Hank helped her serve the men.

"Why didn't you tell me what was going on?" Maggie whispered. "I could've gotten some tablecloths and centerpieces ready."

"All taken care of. The florist you called in Denver has made centerpieces for each table and we rented tablecloths along with the tables."

She noticed a long table at one end, which could be used for cake and punch. Already her mind was dealing with the changes. But it would've helped if she'd had some warning.

An hour later, there was another arrival, one Maggie liked a lot better. A station wagon appeared, its doors opened and five ladies got out. They were all dressed in jeans and shirts, but they carried nice clothes on hangers and overnight bags.

Maggie met them at the door. "Hello?"

"Maggie, it's me, Melanie," a young blonde said. "We thought we'd come early and help. Is that all right?"

"Oh, yes, it's very definitely all right. I think you're saving my life."

After brief introductions, Maggie showed the women to a guest bedroom, the one Kate had used, to put down their things. Then she offered each a cup of coffee before they all got to work.

"I can't tell you how much I appreciate your help," she said.

"We're just glad to meet you," Melanie said. "We heard that Hank had finally hired a housekeeper, but we didn't hear anything else about it. The next thing we heard, Carl was marrying."

"Yes, it surprised all of us," Becky Seward

added. "We hadn't been sure he would even survive."

"He recovered fairly quickly once I started taking care of him."

"I heard Hank's cooking was the worst," another lady, Violet Green, said.

"I would be a failure at running a ranch," Maggie pointed out, protective of Hank even when she was mad at him.

"How true," the fourth lady, Imajean Griffith, said. "And my husband says he's one of the best ranchers around. George is ten years older than Hank, but he asks his opinion on anything he's unsure of."

"So, what do we need to do first?" Becky asked.

Guests had already begun arriving when Carl and Kate arrived with the flowers.

Maggie, dressed for the wedding, rushed out of the house to greet them.

Hank was standing under the awning talking with some of his friends. He noted her long legs, usually hidden by jeans, her small waist and her flowing hair.

"Who's the beauty?" one of his friends asked.

"Yeah, I haven't seen her around before.

I'd like to get her name and her phone number," Jack Horne said. Jack was well-known in the neighborhood as being a ladies' man.

Reluctantly, Hank said, "She's my housekeeper."

"Whoa! She doesn't look like any housekeeper I've ever seen," Roy said. "How's it working out?" Roy displayed a leer conveying his X-rated thoughts.

"She's a terrific housekeeper and I don't want to hear any more remarks like that!" Hank exclaimed, a big scowl on his face. "Excuse me."

He strode across the front lawn toward his dad's car. As his father got out of the car, Hank was there to give him a hug. The two of them went around and helped Kate out of the car. Then Hank hugged Kate, too. His gaze met Maggie's and he smiled, hoping she'd smile back.

"I thought you were getting here earlier," he asked.

"Maggie just said the same thing. But we had to pick up the flowers, son. Can you help me unload them?"

"Of course, Dad. Where are we taking them?"

Maggie stepped forward. "Take them into

the kitchen, please. The ladies will help me get the centerpieces on the tables."

"You've met some of the neighbors?" Kate asked.

"Yes, they came over this morning bright and early to help me. They're wonderful. I'll introduce you to them later. I don't know if we'll have much time for socializing before the wedding."

The two women walked, arm-in-arm, toward the back porch.

Hank and his dad stood staring after them.

"Son, I appreciate you greeting Kate the way you did. She worries about us."

Hank turned to look at his father. "Dad, you know I'm slow to adjust to changes, but I'm getting there. And lately, I see so many similarities between Kate and Maggie."

Carl frowned. "I'm glad, Hank, but I don't really understand what Maggie has to do with it."

Shock registered on Hank's face. "I—I can't explain—I mean, she's so easy to live—I mean, she's easy to—she and Timmy fill the house with love."

Carl studied his son's face for a minute. Then he said softly, "I think that's what first reached out to me. That and Maggie's wonderful cooking. I mean she cared."

"I cared!"

"I know you did, son, but there's something about the opposite sex. Anyway, have things changed between you and Maggie?"

"No! No, nothing's changed. But I appreciate her abilities…and Timmy is the greatest kid." Hank only hoped his father didn't ask Maggie about their relationship.

"You might start thinking about marriage and a family, son. And Maggie would be a good choice for you."

"Dad! I'm not…we're not…" Hank shrugged his shoulders.

"Don't worry, Hank," Carl said, patting his son's shoulder. "I'm going in and get dressed for the wedding. You look nice, by the way."

"Thanks, Dad. I'm entertaining the early arrivals, so I'll be out here. Just yell if you need me."

The two men parted company and Hank headed back to the awning where a number of people were sitting at the tables. He wanted to be sure to be there when Maggie started bringing out the centerpieces. He wanted to protect her from any rude comments or advances from his single buddies. He owed her that at least.

When he reached the front lawn, he saw Maggie. She and two of the ladies helping her were carrying the small centerpieces that would go on each table in box-lid trays.

Immediately Jack and a couple of the other men cornered Maggie.

Hank walked swiftly toward the little crowd.

"Here now, sugar, we're just being friendly," Jack was telling her, trying to slip an arm around her waist.

"Jack!" Hank shouted.

His friend looked up, but Maggie didn't bother. She said something in a low voice and Jack stepped back at once.

Maggie continued delivering the flowers. When she started back to the house, Hank fell in with her.

"What did you say to Jack?"

"I asked him to release me," Maggie said calmly.

"That wouldn't do it with Jack," Hank replied. He'd seen the guy's persistent approach with ladies before.

"Well, I did add that I'd put one of the centerpieces down his pants. He didn't seem to like that idea."

Hank burst out laughing. When she sent him a droll look, he put an arm around her and dropped a kiss on her lips, surprising both of them.

"Uh, sorry, I—I got caught up in the moment."

Maggie didn't meet his gaze. "Yes, of course. Don't think anything about it." Without a backward glance, she hurried into the house.

Realizing he'd kissed her in front of some of the guests, Hank hurriedly looked around to see if anyone had noticed. There were no startled glances, no long stares. He breathed a sign of relief.

Maggie knocked on Kate's door. The other ladies had dressed hurriedly when Kate and Carl had arrived, so Kate could have some privacy.

"Come in," Kate called, "unless you're Carl."

"I'm not," Maggie said with a grin as she opened the door. "Oh, Kate, you look beautiful!"

"Thank you, Maggie. I'm just a little nervous."

"Why?"

"It's been so long since I've lived with anyone."

Maggie started to speak, but Kate continued. "Oh, I don't mean the intimacy thing. It's just that I'm used to getting my own way."

"You'll be fine, Kate. Remember how generous and kind you were when Timmy and I moved in with you."

"You were easy. We're so much alike."

"But Timmy isn't."

"No, but having a child around was fun. By the way, where is Timmy? I haven't seen him since we arrived."

"One of my helper's husbands just arrived with their children. She has a son Timmy's age and they're playing computer games together."

"How nice! It's good for Timmy to make friends here. When he starts school, he won't be so frightened."

"If we're still here then," Maggie said in a subdued voice.

"What are you saying?"

"Well, when you and Carl come back from your honeymoon, you won't need me to keep this house in order. I'll be superfluous."

"No, you won't. I don't want to keep house full-time. Carl and I are planning on traveling quite a bit. I'm not putting you out of a job, Maggie. And besides, aren't you happy here?"

"Yes, but Hank…he made a secret deal with Timmy, without telling me."

"The one you mentioned last time?" Kate asked, frowning.

"We don't need to worry about it now. You are getting married in a few minutes."

"There's time. Tell me."

Maggie sat down, twisting her hands together. "Hank said I was holding Timmy too close. He told Timmy he could sleep in his old bedroom. And he offered him a puppy to sleep with him so he wouldn't get scared."

"He shouldn't have done that without talking to you first," Kate said. "But it is time for Timmy to stop sharing your room."

"I know. I was furious with Hank…but I've realized he's right. And Timmy will make the move much more willingly with the reward of a puppy, which, by the way, he named Wiggles as he will tell you ad nauseum."

"So you've forgiven Hank?"

"I'm working on it. But he isn't to make decisions for my son without talking to me.

He has no children. What makes him think he knows best?"

"I agree. And he should understand how—how frightening that is for you."

"Yes," Maggie agreed, thinking other things could be frightening, also, like a surprise kiss from a drop-dead gorgeous rancher like Hank.

"Well, I've taken up enough of your time. Let's get you married, Aunt Kate."

"Oh, I can't wait. You know, my first husband and I eloped, and I never had a proper wedding. When I told Carl that, he was determined I would have a fairy-tale kind of wedding this time. He even wanted me to buy a traditional long gown, but I drew the line there."

Maggie smiled as she admired Kate's white silk suit, topped by a small hat and a piece of white veiling that covered her eyes. "You look terrific."

They came out of the room together. When they reached the kitchen, they found Timmy sitting at the table with his new friend. Melanie, his friend's mother, was supervising them until Maggie arrived.

Kate hugged Timmy, after Maggie checked

his hands. Then they all moved to the front door. Melanie took her son to join her husband and little girl. With a wave from Maggie, another lady turned on a taped recording of the wedding march.

When the music began, Timmy stepped out and walked toward the temporary altar where Hank and Carl waited. Since he hadn't seen Carl since his arrival, he waved to him and said hi. The crowd laughed, which startled Timmy.

When the little boy stopped and stared around him, Hank called softly, "It's okay, Tim. Come stand by me."

Timmy almost ran to safety beside Hank.

Maggie had followed Timmy. She wore a soft turquoise silk dress and a string of pearls around her neck. Hank thought she looked elegant, but fragile. She looked so beautiful, he thought. Could this possibly be the same feisty young widow that had taken over his home…and his heart?

It was only when the crowd stood for Kate's arrival that Hank remembered that this was Carl's wedding. It had been so easy to focus on Maggie.

He stood opposite Maggie with his father

and Kate between them. His gaze met hers across the altar and she demurely looked down. What had he done to embarrass her? Then he remembered the sweet kiss he'd stolen. He'd have to add that to the mistakes he'd made with her.

Immediately after the ceremony, while Larry took several pictures of the bride and groom, Maggie and her ladies brought out the food and drinks to the tables. Hank and one of his friends carried out the wedding cake and returned for the groom's cake.

As soon as the guests settled down to eating, Kate and Carl called for Timmy, Maggie and Hank to join them in a family portrait. Larry snapped plenty of pictures. Then he suggested he make several of the best man and the maid of honor. Hank slid his hand around Maggie's waist and pulled her close. When she resisted after the first picture, Hank whispered to her the necessity of closeness in the photos. The pictures would make a nice memory for Carl and Kate of their big day.

Before long the picture-taking was finished and it was time for Kate and Carl to cut the wedding cake.

Maggie breathed a sigh of relief. Several of Hank's friends were filling champagne glasses for those who wanted it. Other guests were being served the punch.

"Mommy, why is the chocolate cake Carl's cake? Won't he share?" Timmy asked.

"I guess he'd better since you and Hank like chocolate so much," Maggie answered. She assured her son that Carl would share. She led him over to stand near the cake until after Carl had cut the first piece.

"Is this a line?" Hank asked, whispering in Maggie's ear.

She jumped, surprised by his approach. "Uh, yes. Timmy wants chocolate cake. Could you see that he gets it? I need to replenish several of the serving dishes."

Hank frowned. "Sure, but you're supposed to enjoy the wedding, too."

But Maggie had already slipped away. She was not eager to have the neighbors see her and Hank whispering together.

The afternoon flowed smoothly as Carl and Kate greeted their guests and moved from table to table for Kate to meet more of Carl's friends. Laughter floated in the air. Timmy and several other young children raced around the perimeter of the awning.

Hank continued to play host, making sure everyone had whatever they needed. He was teased repeatedly about his beautiful young housekeeper, but he didn't mind as long as Maggie didn't hear any of the remarks.

Unbeknownst to him, Maggie was receiving her share of comments, particularly about how she'd lucked into a job for the area's most eligible bachelor. As one woman explained, there were other bachelors, of course, but none as popular as Hank. Only since his mother died had he withdrawn from an active social life.

The ladies encouraged her to get him to socialize more. Maggie tried to respond with noncommittal responses. She was strangely reluctant to push Hank into social activities with other women. When she realized what she was thinking, she hurried to the house on the pretense that she needed to check on something.

Inside, in the kitchen, she stood staring out the window.

"Maggie? Is something wrong?" Melanie asked.

"Oh! I—I thought there were more quiches in here, but we seem to be out of them."

"Of course, we are. Those men have gobbled up everything you've prepared. I think if you look for another job in the area, you'll have a lot of offers."

"Not if their wives see her first," Becky said with a laugh as she entered the kitchen. "I bet your social life is about to improve, too. Our local bachelors are all abuzz about you."

"Oh, no! I mean… I have Timmy."

"A little boy can't take the place of a man, honey," Becky assured her. "I mean, I have four kids, but I send them all to a movie so my husband and I can be alone. You know what I mean?"

Melanie stepped forward. "I think she knows what you mean, Becky, but Maggie is sort of losing her aunt, her only family, today. It takes some adjustment."

"Well, I think—" Becky started.

But Maggie said, "I think the new pot of coffee is ready. Could you take it out, Becky? I'll follow with the cream and sugar."

"Of course I can," Becky said and immediately picked up the oversized pot and hurried outside.

"She means well," Melanie said quietly.

"I know. But you're right. Things are changing."

Something in her voice disturbed Melanie. "You're not thinking of leaving, are you?"

"No, not necessarily, but when Kate and Carl come back, they won't need me here. I'm not sure how things will work out."

Melanie began fixing a tray with cream and sugar. "Let me know if I can help. I was hoping we could arrange some play dates for Tim and Billy."

"I'd love that. Tim needs to get used to playing with other children."

"Well, silly me. I didn't think to tell you about Mother's Day Out at the church in town. Mondays and Thursdays, from nine to three, the kids play, have a few lessons and a nap. He'll need a mat for his nap, but they provide lunch and it only costs seven dollars per child. Billy goes every week. He loves it!"

"Oh, Melanie, thanks for telling me. I'll sign Timmy up at once. Or do I need to apply first?"

"Nope. Just bring him. I'll call a friend who works there and let her know he's coming. And you can get a mat for him at the general store in town."

"Thanks, Melanie," Maggie said, thinking how nice it would be to have the other woman for a friend.

Chapter 12

"Maggie?" Hank's voice penetrated the walls of the kitchen.

"That sounds urgent," Melanie commented.

"Yes, I'd better go see what disaster has occurred."

"I'll come with you. Maybe I can help."

Maggie was pleased to have Melanie's company. Especially when she discovered the reason for the loud summons. "Hank, what is it?" she asked at once.

"Kate wants you here to join the ladies waiting for her to throw the bouquet."

Maggie stared at him. Then she said, "Oh,

no, I'm not—I mean, I think it's for ladies who haven't been married."

"Maybe," he assured her, "but Kate wants you in there."

Maggie looked in Kate's direction, unable to ignore the frantic waving. She hurried to Kate's side and whispered, "Kate, I don't think this is a good idea."

"It's just for fun, Maggie. Please, just for me?" Kate pleaded.

Her aunt looked so happy, Maggie couldn't deny her anything. She slipped to the back of the group of young women and waited.

With her back to them, Kate hefted her bouquet high in the air, aiming for Maggie's location. Maggie intentionally moved to one side, getting out of the way of those who were seriously pursuing the prize. One woman reached out for the bouquet and popped it right into Maggie's hand. She had reached up on reflex, but suddenly she found herself the prizewinner.

Everyone clapped and surrounded Maggie and Kate. Larry hurried to photograph the bride and the winner.

Next, it was Carl's turn to toss the garter, after removing it from Kate's thigh. The single men gathered, most of them looking rather reluctant to win the prize since it meant they'd soon be walking down the aisle themselves. Even Hank was in the group, Maggie noted.

Much to her surprise, Hank retrieved the garter, though he had to jump several feet in the air to do so. Larry took a picture of Hank and his father. Then he suggested the wedding couple and the two winners. Hank put the two women in the middle and him and his father on the ends. He immediately put his arm around Maggie.

"People can see, Hank," she whispered, thinking her words would make him move away.

"It's for the pictures," he whispered in return.

Then Larry suggested a picture of Maggie holding the bouquet and Hank with the garter on his coat sleeve. With half their neighbors looking on, Maggie had little choice but to comply. As soon as the picture was taken, she began moving among their guests, offering coffee or more food. Melanie and Becky were putting the remains of the wedding cake in an appropriate box for freezing.

As Maggie moved quietly around, she heard comments about the fact that she and

Hank won the tosses, as if it were planned. Cringing at those words, she tried to keep her distance from Hank.

Then Carl and Kate began their goodbyes.

She hurried to Kate's side, hugging her and wishing her the best in the world.

"I wish the same for you, honey," Kate assured her, returning her hug.

Maggie's only response was a smile. Timmy, jumping up and down beside her, couldn't wait to hug his Aunt Kate. After he did so, Maggie pulled him back, holding his hand. Carl stepped to her side and kissed her cheek. Then he picked up Timmy and hugged him.

"While I'm gone, just ask Hank if you need anything," Carl said to both of them. "He's promised to take care of you two."

"We can take care of ourselves, Carl. We hope you and Kate have a lovely time on your cruise."

"I'm sure we will. We'll call when we can."

As soon as he and Kate left, the crowd began to thin rapidly. Maggie seemed to say goodbye to someone every other minute. Each of them had a word of advice for her.

They ranged from "call us if you need anything," to "good luck with the wedding thing," to "grab him while he's home alone with you!" The last came from Becky on her way out the door.

Fortunately, Maggie didn't have to answer her.

Because she didn't have an answer in her own head.

She admired Hank. He'd done all he could to help his father, which told her that family was important to him.

She could admire that in a man. But was she ready to risk her heart or her son's future?

Melanie brought in a second tray of cups and plates.

"Oh, Melanie, you don't have to do that," Maggie told her. "I have all evening to clean up."

"It will go faster with two of us. Actually, four of us, because I organized Hank and Ben. They're going to bring in the rest of the cups and saucers and champagne glasses. We'll be finished in no time."

"You are such a dear!" Maggie exclaimed. They began loading the dishwasher together. Then they ran water in the sink and began washing and drying by hand.

They had almost finished when the two

men came in with two trays piled high with dirty dishware.

"Are we sure we want to thank them?" Melanie asked.

"I believe we do. After all, we didn't have to go out and pick up all of those dirty dishes." Maggie asked the two men to put the trays on the table.

"Should Ben and I start loading the boxes with what you've cleaned?" Hank asked.

Maggie looked at him for the first time since she'd come in the house. "That would be nice, if you don't mind."

"We don't mind," Ben replied. "But we do expect a reward when we've finished."

Melanie laughed at her husband's response, but Maggie avoided Hank's gaze.

An hour later, when Hank and Ben had loaded all the packed boxes into Hank's truck, Hank invited Ben and his family to stay for dinner.

"I'll throw some steaks on the grill. The girls will only have to make some vegetables. And there's plenty of chocolate cake left for dessert."

"Sounds good to me if you're sure Maggie won't mind."

The two men came back to the kitchen

and Hank repeated his invitation to Melanie and Maggie.

Melanie protested at once. "Oh, no, we couldn't. Maggie's had a long day already."

"Hank's right, Melanie. It won't take much cooking on our part. I'd love to see Hank cook for once."

"Will you make your whipped potatoes?" Hank asked.

"If that's what you want. And we can steam some broccoli. That won't take much time." Maggie began organizing the kitchen for the evening meal. "But your little girl. What will she eat?"

"Steak and potatoes will please her," Melanie said.

"Oh, I know. I have some cans of fruit salad. We can add some whipped cream, and I know she'll like it."

"So will Billy. He has such a sweet tooth. Does Tim?"

"Sometimes. He's begun to emulate Hank, wanting chocolate." Maggie suddenly looked around. "Where are the kids?"

Hank answered. "They're in the family room watching a movie. I thought it would keep them out of your hair."

"That's so thoughtful," Melanie said,

smiling at Hank. "I wish Ben thought about things like that."

"With another child on the way, maybe you'd better coach him," Maggie said, and then giggled.

"At least you've got one who doesn't need coaching," Melanie returned, laughing. Her laughter faded away at the distraught look on Maggie's face.

"Maggie, I'm sorry. I didn't mean—"

Hank stepped up and put an arm around Maggie's shoulders. "Don't worry, Melanie. Maggie's just a little shy."

"You mean you have an announcement?" Melanie asked, delight in her voice.

"No!" Maggie exclaimed. "No, we are employer-employee. That's all." She turned away, peeling potatoes in the sink, as if she were alone.

Melanie mouthed "I'm sorry" to Hank and began washing the broccoli. Hank took steaks out of the freezer.

"We're going out to start the grill. I figure the steaks will be done in half an hour."

Maggie tossed over her shoulder, "Tim and I like ours cooked medium-well."

"Yes, ma'am." Hank gave a little salute as he went out the back door, followed by Ben.

"I'm sorry, Maggie. I didn't mean to embarrass you," Melanie said softly.

"You didn't. Hank just—there's nothing between us." Maggie kept her head down and peeled the potatoes.

"But I saw him kiss you!" Melanie exclaimed. "That's why I thought—"

"I said something that pleased him. He was just being playful, that's all."

"Oh, of course."

The rest of the evening went well. Dinner was a big success, according to Tim and Billy. Even Ashley, Melanie's daughter, enjoyed the meal. Ben agreed with Hank that Maggie's potatoes were the best.

After dinner, while the boys played a video game and Ashley fell asleep in her mother's lap, the four adults lingered over cups of coffee.

When Ben and Melanie rose to go, they both expressed their enjoyment of the evening. Maggie and Hank thanked them for their assistance. Melanie reminded Maggie about Mother's Day Out on Monday.

Maggie, Hank and Tim waved goodbye as the family drove away.

"You're taking Tim to Mother's Day Out?" Hank asked, sounding surprised.

"Yes, I am. Do I need your approval?" Maggie asked sharply.

"No, of course not."

"What's Mother's Day Out?" Timmy asked his mother.

"It's a place where you and Billy can play and learn some things to get you ready for real school." Maggie took his hand. "Won't that be fun?"

"Okay. Billy will be there?"

"Yes, he will. Now it's time for you to go to bed," Maggie said, leading the way to their room.

"Wait, Mommy!" Timmy protested, digging in his heels. "I get to sleep in Hank's little-boy room, don't I?"

"Yeah, I agree," Hank said.

"But you don't have—that is, I haven't made up the bed for you yet. I'll do that tomorrow."

"But, Mommy—"

"Your mom is right, Tim. She's had a long day. We'll let her slide tonight. And tomorrow, I think it will be time for Wiggles to leave his mom, too. Then the two of you will be together."

"Oh, boy!" Timmy exclaimed. For the next half hour, Maggie had to listen to Timmy talking about Wiggles and Hank's old room. When she finally got him settled, she slipped out of the bedroom with a sigh.

"You worn out?" Hank asked softly. He was still lingering in the kitchen.

"I'm worn out by listening to stories about Wiggles and what he and my son are going to do. I never even agreed to such a thing."

"But, Maggie—"

"Don't start, Hank. I just couldn't handle an argument tonight."

"No, I won't argue with you. Instead, I have a surprise for you."

"What?"

"A friend of mine filmed the wedding today. I thought you might like to see it."

Her eyes lit up. "Really? I'd love to see it."

"Right this way, my lady," Hank said with a grin.

They went into the family room. He sat her down on the sofa and went to put the videotape in the machine.

With her gaze eagerly fixed on the television screen, Maggie scarcely noticed that Hank sat beside her. She was leaning forward, waiting for the tape to begin.

For the next half hour, they relived the wedding of their relatives. As the tape ended,

Maggie leaned back. When she felt Hank's arm around her, she jerked away. "I—I'll see you in the morning," she said, jumping to her feet.

Hank stood, too. "Wait a minute. We need to discuss the fact that I kissed you today."

"No! No, we don't have to discuss it. I realize it was an impulsive act. It didn't mean anything!"

"You're wrong, Maggie," Hank said, holding her by her shoulders. "It meant a lot to me." Without warning, his lips covered hers for another kiss, this one longer and deeper.

When he finally lifted his lips from hers, he held her tightly against him. "Honey, I've been wanting to do that for a long time, only I was afraid you'd never speak to me again if I did."

"I shouldn't," she whispered.

"Why? Have you given your heart to someone else?"

She shook her head no.

He tipped her chin up so she looked at him. "Maggie, I never intended to fall in love with you. I thought you just got under my skin because you were so ornery," he said, grinning at her. "Then I started thinking about what it would be like if you left. I realized I couldn't stand that."

"There are other cooks, Hank," Maggie said, closing her eyes.

"I know that. And I'll hire one if you want me to, like maybe when you're pregnant."

Maggie pushed him away. "What are you talking about? We aren't—I'm not—This is a ridiculous discussion."

"Okay, maybe I'm ahead of the game, but I've thought about you being pregnant with my child. Our child. A brother for Tim, or a little sister."

"When did you start thinking about all of this?" she asked, still startled by his words.

"When I realized I didn't want you to go away, or to date anyone but me. I knew I should marry you, so we could be a family. You, me, Tim and any other babies we have. Tim needs a daddy, Maggie."

"Don't you think you've made this decision awfully quickly?"

"No. I think from the first minute I saw you, I fell for you, but there were so many other emotions going on inside me that I couldn't accept my feelings. You snuck up on me."

"*I* snuck up on *you?*" she almost shrieked.

"I wasn't trying to trap you. I was trying to help you get over your mother's death."

"I know and...thank you. You know what Dad said to me? He said he responded to your cooking because he could tell you cared. Well, I could tell the same thing even though I was arguing with you. It's probably a good thing that we didn't realize what was happening until now, because it would've been awkward around here with Dad and Kate."

"Hank, I don't think—"

"Are you telling me you don't care about me? That wasn't what I felt when I kissed you."

Her cheeks flamed, but she didn't look away. "I'll admit I'm attracted to you, Hank, but that doesn't mean we're getting married."

"Why not?"

"I'm not sure you're prepared to become a daddy."

"I think I am. That's why I wanted Tim to move into my room. He needs to become more independent. He also needs a man in his life."

"He's only four!" she exclaimed.

Hank drew her back into his body. "If he's sleeping in my old room, it won't bother him so much that you're sleeping with me."

"I didn't say I was!"

He kissed her again. This time, Maggie couldn't hold back the attraction she'd felt from the very beginning. He'd gotten under her guard because he'd been in such pain, and he'd cared so much about his dad. His kisses were addictive, and she was losing control.

After about five minutes of such close communication, Hank pushed her away. "We've got to stop."

"Uh, yes, we should."

"You need to go to sleep with Timmy. And I'll see you in the morning."

"Yes, all right," she said, barely able to think after his kisses.

He put his arm around her and walked her to the door of her room. After another quick kiss, he pushed her through the door and shut it after her.

Maggie leaned against the door, her head still spinning. She hadn't believed Hank had any interest in her at all. Only in the last few days had he shown any attention to her. Before, he seemed only interested in Timmy.

She couldn't hold back a smile at what she suspected Timmy's reaction would be to having Hank for a daddy.

Not that she was counting on Hank feeling

the same way in the morning. Perhaps he'd lost his head as a result of all the emotion of Kate and Carl's very romantic wedding. Maybe he'd had a little too much champagne. No, she wouldn't be surprised if he came to the breakfast table and ignored her.

But she'd be hurt. Desperately hurt.

That thought was enough to send her scurrying to the bed, seeking sleep to drown out such depressing thoughts.

Breakfast wasn't served until eight on Sunday mornings. Hank woke up around seven, a little later than usual. He lay in bed for some time thinking about sharing his bed, his life, with Maggie.

Then he headed for the kitchen and put on a pot of coffee to have it ready for Maggie. He sat down with his first cup a few minutes later, waiting for her appearance.

When she stumbled into the kitchen at seven-thirty, he watched her cross the kitchen to the coffeepot, not even noticing him. She picked up the pot and then put it down again.

"It's already done, Maggie," he said softly.

She whirled around to stare at him.

"Sit down, honey, and I'll pour you some coffee. You look like you could use some."

He stood and guided her to a chair next to his. Then he poured her some coffee and set it in front of her.

"Thank you. You surprised me."

"You could've slept in, if you wanted. Want to go back to bed?"

"No! No, I'm fine. The coffee will help."

"Good." He bent down and dropped a kiss on her lips before he took his seat again.

Maggie shot him a troubling look. "You haven't changed your mind?"

"About marrying you and Timmy? Of course not."

She took another deep sip of coffee.

When she said nothing, Hank asked, "Have you?"

"I never promised—no, but I'm not sure— Hank, it's all so sudden."

"We can wait until Kate and Dad return to have the wedding. I'm a reasonable man."

She couldn't help but laugh. "Oh, yes, you're incredibly reasonable, aren't you?"

He leaned over and kissed her. "I love to see you happy," he whispered. Then he kissed her again, a longer, deeper, more passionate kiss.

"Hey! Why are you kissing Mommy?" Timmy asked from the door.

"Because I love her. Is that okay?" Hank asked calmly.

"Yeah, I guess so. If she doesn't mind. It looks kinda yucky to me," Timmy said, as he crawled into his usual chair. "I'm hungry, Mommy."

"Uh, right, I'll start breakfast. Do you two want pancakes?" The two men in her life nodded in unison.

She kept her back to both of them while she started the bacon cooking and mixed up the pancake batter. Her son entertained Hank with numerous observations about his dog, Wiggles.

"Your mom hasn't said you could have Wiggles, has she?"

"Didn't you, Mommy?" Timmy cried out in panic. "I promise I'll be very good!"

"You're not the only one who has to promise," Maggie said, turning to stare at the two of them. "Hank has to promise to help you train that puppy. I'm not going to change your sheets every day because the dog doesn't know any better."

"Your mom has a point there. I promise to help him train his puppy. And I'll help him learn how to take care of Wiggles, right, Tim?"

"Yes, sir," Tim said, responding to the command in his voice.

"See, Mom? All taken care of."

"I'm not your mom," she pointed out.

"True. Shall we tell Timmy?"

Maggie whirled around. "No! Not until we're sure!"

"Tell me what?" Timmy asked, his gaze going from one adult to the other.

"I'm sure," Hank told her, his gaze steady.

"I—I—you said we could wait until—"

"Wait for what?" Timmy asked more anxiously.

"Your mom and I were thinking about getting married, too, if you wouldn't mind me being your daddy," Hank said casually, though he watched the boy closely.

"That'd be okay with me," Timmy said. "I'd like having a daddy. Billy has a daddy."

"So he does. He also has a little sister. Want one of those, too?"

Timmy pursed his lips. Then he said, "Well, maybe. I'd like a brother better."

"I'm partial to boys, too," Hank said, "but a little girl might be nice."

"Excuse me for interrupting, but eat your breakfast," Maggie ordered both of them as she slapped their plates onto the table.

"Is she mad?" Timmy whispered to Hank.

"Nope. She's just fussy this morning because we worked so hard yesterday. We'll do the dishes for her after breakfast so she can relax. Then she'll feel better."

"You think I'm that easy?" she demanded.

"Yeah," Hank said with a grin before he kissed her again.

"Are you gonna do that all the time?" Timmy asked with a scowl.

"Yeah. That's what moms and dads do, buddy."

"Okay," Timmy agreed with a disgusted sigh. "After we do the dishes, can we go to the barn and get Wiggles?"

"Sounds like a plan. Maybe your mom would like to go with us?"

"Would you, Mommy? You could meet Wiggles!"

"Yes, of course, sweetie."

They all ate in silence for a few minutes. Then Timmy looked at Hank. "Do I get to call Carl Grandpa?"

"Do you want to?" Hank asked.

"Yeah. Billy has a grandpa, too."

"Then I definitely think you should call him Grandpa," Hank said with a grin.

The phone rang, and Maggie gasped. She

stared at Hank as he reached for the phone. "Hi, Dad. How's it going?"

Timmy slipped from his chair. "I want to talk to him," he pleaded.

Hank held him off for a minute. Then he told his father Timmy had something to say to him.

"Timmy, don't—" Maggie gasped, finally realizing why her son wanted to speak to Carl.

"Hi, Grandpa!" Timmy listened for a minute and then passed the phone back to Hank and returned to his breakfast.

"What did Carl say?"

"He said hi. Then he wanted to talk to Hank again."

Unconcerned, Timmy continued to eat his pancakes.

Maggie stared at Hank. When he held the phone out to her, he said, "Kate wants to say hi."

"Maggie, is it true? Are you and Hank going to marry?"

"Uh, we're talking about it?"

"I told Carl I thought you were in love with each other!" Kate exclaimed. "I'm so happy for you."

"Kate, it's been so fast, I'm not—"

"That's the way it takes us sometime. You never know how much time you'll have, honey. Go for it."

"Are you having a good time?"

"Yes, but we're coming back sooner than we'd planned. We'll be there to stay with Timmy after you and Hank marry."

"Oh, no, don't—"

"Carl wants to talk to Hank again," Kate said and suddenly Carl was on the phone.

Maggie gave the phone to Hank and sat back down at the table.

After Hank hung up the phone, he sat down and took Maggie's hand. "Honey, am I rushing you too much?"

"I—I love you, Hank, but it's scary. I don't want to suffer again."

"You sound like my dad talking."

Maggie's eyes widened. "I do?"

"Yeah, and I agreed with him, until I realized I couldn't live without you and Timmy in my life. Could you leave here and be happy?"

Slowly, Maggie shook her head.

"Buddy, why don't you go to the barn and get Larry to take you to Wiggles. Tell him I'll be out after I finish the dishes," Hank said to Timmy.

"Okay, Mommy?" the boy dutifully asked.

Maggie nodded her head and Timmy was quickly out the door.

Then Hank took Maggie's hand and pulled her out of her chair and into his lap. He was pleased when her arms slid around his neck. "We're going to be happy, Maggie. I promise I'll take care of you and Timmy, and I'll love only you, as long as I live."

She covered his lips with her hands. "No, don't even mention such a thing."

"Okay. Do you believe me?"

"Yes, I do."

"Practice those words." He kissed her and for the first time, she gave everything she had to the kiss. After several minutes, Hank pushed her off his lap. "I've got to go to the barn and check on Timmy."

"Okay." She didn't even mention that he'd forgotten he'd promised to wash the dishes.

"Oh, and honey," he said as he paused by the back door.

"What?"

"Make up the bed in the guest room, please."

"Are we having company?"

"Yeah, Larry's going to be staying with us until Dad and Kate get back. I don't trust myself alone with you after Timmy's gone to bed."

Hank strode out the door and off the porch, his long legs eating up the space between the house and the barn.

Maggie stood there, a smile on her lips as she watched her man go to her son. He would make Timmy a wonderful father. But he'd make her an even better husband. He was already a family man. One she could trust to love her and her son.

A man she could love with all her heart.

*   *   *   *   *